THE CHERRY TREE

ADRIAN BELL was born in 1902, and began a career as a journalist on the *Observer* before tiring of London life and becoming apprenticed to a West Suffolk farmer of the old school. In 1921 he bought thirty-five acres of his own land at Stradishall, and continued to farm in East Anglia until after the Second World War.

He contributed a weekly column about country life to the *Eastern Daily Press* for thirty-five years, and many of these essays were published in book form. The first volume of his autobiographical trilogy, *Corduroy,* appeared in 1930, to be followed by *Silver Ley* and *The Cherry Tree*. These books at once established for him a high literary reputation. He also compiled crosswords for *The Times* for half a century. He died in 1980.

HUMPHREY PHELPS was born in 1927, the son and grandson of Gloucestershire farmers, and has spent all his life on a farm. He is married, with three sons and two grandchildren, and now has a two-hundred-acre mixed farm run on traditional lines.

Since the first in 1974, he has published eight books, including *Just Across the Fields* (1976), a story of farming and country life in the 1940s. This was followed by *Just Over Yonder* (1977), *Just Where We Belong* (1978), and *The Forest of Dean* (1982). His latest book is *Uncle George and Company*.

ALSO AVAILABLE IN
TWENTIETH-CENTURY CLASSICS

ADRIAN BELL

The Cherry Tree

INTRODUCED BY

HUMPHREY PHELPS

Oxford   New York

OXFORD UNIVERSITY PRESS

1985

NOTE

*None of the characters in this book is to be
regarded as the portrait of a living person.*

Oxford University Press, Walton Street, Oxford OX2 6DP

*Oxford New York Toronto
Delhi Bombay Calcutta Madras Karachi
Petaling Jaya Singapore Hong Kong Tokyo
Nairobi Dar es Salaam Cape Town
Melbourne Auckland*

*and associated companies in
Beirut Berlin Ibadan Nicosia*

Oxford is a trade mark of Oxford University Press

*First published 1932 by John Lane The Bodley Head
First issued, with Humphrey Phelps's introduction, as an
Oxford University Press paperback 1985
Reprinted 1986*

British Library Cataloguing in Publication Data
*Bell, Adrian
The Cherry tree.—(Twentieth-century classics)
1. Country life—England—Suffolk
2. Suffolk—Social life and customs
I. Title II. Series
942.6'4083'0924 S522.G7
ISBN 0–19–281879–1*

Library of Congress Cataloging in Publication Data
*Bell, Adrian, 1901–
The cherry tree.
(Twentieth-century classics)
First published: J. Lane, Bodley Head, 1932.
I. Title II. Series
PR6003.E423C4 1985 823'.912 85–263
ISBN 0–19 281879–1 (pbk.)*

*Printed in Great Britain by
Richard Clay (The Chaucer Press) Ltd.
Bungay, Suffolk*

INTRODUCTION

BY HUMPHREY PHELPS

The Cherry Tree is the final volume of Adrian Bell's famous Suffolk trilogy, begun with *Corduroy* and *Silver Ley*. Together, written in Bell's characteristically fine prose, they tell the story of a town boy's transformation into a countryman and record the ways of a now vanished rural world and of the old system of farming. Though I say *fine* I will not say *finest* for that implies comparison, and the work of Adrian Bell is incomparable. There have been other good rural writers but Adrian Bell is unique. In his books, he does not merely record, but recreates the substance and sensations of a living, working world—a world now dead but one which lives perennially in his pages and one in which we too feel we are living and working. We can hear the rustle of the sheaves and the rumble of the wagons in the harvest field; smell the scent of the newly-ploughed earth, the sweat of the horses, the steaming dung-hill. No, this is no mere record, this really is rural life and work, authentic in every detail, truth shining with beauty.

It was good fortune which sent Adrian Bell, fleeing from London and the threat of an office life, into Suffolk in 1920. It was still the time of 'high farming', the rules of good husbandry prevailed, the horse ruled the farm, and the old rural structure was still intact. Soon, and within the period covered by the trilogy, the fabric of this way of life began to crumble.

The volumes of this trilogy were only the first of Adrian Bell's books to enrich English rural literature;

the personal narrative, embodying the quintessence of rural England, is continued in *By Road* (1937), *Apple Acre* (1942), *Sunrise to Sunset* (1944), and *The Budding Morrow* (1947). A different kind of trilogy comprises *The Balcony* (1934), *A Young Man's Fancy* (1955), and *The Mill House* (1958).

Two unautobiographical novels, *The Shepherd's Farm* and *Folly Field*, appeared in the thirties; another, *Music in the Morning* (1954), has been called ' a twentieth-century Cranford'. He published a book of poems in 1934 and another in 1935, and an anthology of English rural life in 1936. There are also several books of essays and the autobiography. Not all his work reaches the peak attained by the Suffolk trilogy, but some, I think, surpasses it, particularly *Men and the Fields*. Neglected for so long, this is happily and deservedly back in print. Judging by this wealth of writing, the time of his arrival in Suffolk was all-important, a tremendous stroke of luck for English rural literature, for us and for generations to come. Credit must also be given to Mr Colville, Bell's mentor at Farley Hall, who taught him those agricultural details of which, as a London refugee in 1920, he knew nothing.

'I am thankful I was born early enough to hear the rumble of harvest wagons,' Bell wrote in an essay fifty years later:

I am glad to have forked sheaves . . . Now I see the rare rhythms of their work, building a round stack broadening from the base like a peg top. What instinct, what an eye for form they had . . . But who can transmit to paper the quiet of their strenuous farming days, or the rhythm of the tread of a dozen horses in plough-trace or shafts, which governed the rhythm of the farm? Or recall its chime of small sounds—ting of pail, spud scraping plough breast, clang of rib-roll, chains jingling as a team swung homeward at the end of the day?

Who indeed but Adrian Bell, who also wrote: 'I like, too, to see the scythes swinging . . . Two scythes swinging are more than twice the beauty of one scythe swinging, because harmony is added to rhythm'? There is rhythm and harmony in his prose, and he captures the rhythm of farm work because he experienced it. Unlike Bell, most, perhaps all, of the other great rural writers were only observers. Because he had forked sheaves, spread muck, ploughed, hoed, and had done all those other countless jobs on the farm, his work has both authenticity and understanding.

As he himself wrote in an essay in 1972, 'Hardy had only a superficial idea of what farm work entailed.' And Bell goes on to say that Richard Jefferies too, in writing about the farm labourer without first-hand experience of farm work, was led to the mistaken conclusion that 'his life and work were animal'. Jefferies and writers like him stated correctly that the farm worker was abominally underpaid and housed, but

without thinking further, because they did not know, they adduced his miserable condition also to the work itself, as rendered the man as animal as his horse. They noticed what a strain it looked for a man to pitch sheaf after sheaf on to a wagon, and the long walk behind plough and horse-hoe, and the jobs of scything (but read Tolstoy who did it), of plying a billhook all day, or using any of the many hand tools of the trade. They were ignorant of the inherent rhythm . . . Now hardly anyone remembers what Hardy and Jefferies and onlookers never divined—namely those rhythms which gave a sort of jollity to the job of using all the tools of farming, so that men could talk and joke as they did it.

Adrian Bell was, as he admitted, a romantic, but a realistic romantic, depicting a range of memorable scenes which are both idyllic and authentic. He found poetry in the stiff obdurate Suffolk clay. As he goes about his work in the fields and barns we feel that we are accompanying him; we too hear the talk of farmers, farmworkers, dealers. We follow and appreciate the cadences and peculiarities of the Suffolk dialect. There is never a false note, never a false move or situation, his sensitivity never descends to sentimentality. The rhythm is always there, the balance is always maintained.

Bell's evocation of his rural world is a considerable achievement, so lightly done that we scarcely notice how considerable it is: so apparently simple and yet so profound. It is a world that he has created, a world with more dimensions than we ever realized; a world in which the common, mundane occurrences and things of everyday life and use are seen to be continually fresh and exciting. Like Walter de la Mare he realized:

> The lovely in life is the familiar,
> And only the lovelier for continuing strange.

And Bell's writing, especially in *The Cherry Tree*, is consistently worthy of comparison with de la Mare's verse:

It was continually with me, as I went about that morning, that such beauty, the bright-worn, manual workaday beauty of what one used, was the light of life for me, though it had not occured to me in those words. For labour, I feel, is the key to satisfying life, the soother of worry, preparing one also for the appreciation of food and rest. If you consider bodily toil primitive and blunting (as you may be justified in doing), then this beauty is a very pedestrian affair, but I confess I am touched always with a sense of mystery at sight of things that flash and shine with use among the mire they move in; it is always a little miracle of transfiguration—ploughshares, iron toe-pieces of men's boots, fork prongs and chains.

This gift to see and to convey his insights to the reader was developed as he continued to write, and in his later books commonplace incidents and moments in time are invested with an irresistible charm and life. Some of these later books have little enough of a story-line; they are essays, snatches of a spiritual autobiography; an incident sets him off thinking, he talks to himself, and the reader is a privileged listener.

INTRODUCTION

In 1961, Adrian Bell published his autobiography, *My Own Master*, which showed that *The Cherry Tree* and its companions were subjected to some selection and adaptation—'gently novelized memoirs' was the phrase used by Ronald Blythe. With this proviso, we can accept the trilogy as autobiography, which is what it essentially is.

By the time *The Cherry Tree* opens, the author has published a book, 'a bull-headed account of my year at Farley Hall'. He has been living at his own farm, Silver Ley, for several years, as a bachelor, but soon he tires of solitude and marries. I do not propose to recount or explain the story you are about to read; to do so would be unnecessary as well as impertinent. It is sufficient to say that Bell has written a love story; of a man and woman starting life together and of their love for the land. As he says, 'There were spheres of influence—mine the farm, Nora's the house—but in the garden they and we met.' Yet this book is more than that, just as the storm that has wrecked the cherry tree—the king of the former orchard—also represents the greater storm of social upheaval, caused by the repeal of the Corn Production Act. Bell does not fantasize when he shows us the effects of the farming depression: ruined fields and barns, ruined farmers and farm workers, dereliction and despair, the crumbling of the rural structure, a different type of farming, different methods and remedies in a desperate situation. Nothing is glossed over, nothing minimized. Yet despite everything this is still a happy book, happy because its many vignettes are truthful and humorous, because its love of life sustains its buoyancy, and because its cheerfullness endures the times of hardship.

It is clear from Adrian Bell's books that a former townsman has produced the classic account of farming. This is not so surprising as it might seem: other townsmen turned countrymen have also produced good, if dissimilar, types of rural writing. The difference is that none became a part of the country in the way that Adrian Bell did. Indeed, many countrymen who have produced good rural books, after extolling the virtues and attractions of the country, hastened to the town at the first opportunity. Bell on the other hand went to Suffolk and remained there.

His complete authenticity and feel for the country have an especial appeal for me. Authenticity in country writing is comparatively rare, for even the most respected writers are guilty of inaccuracy. But never Bell, who had himself performed the routine tasks he describes. He knew that much of real farming—particularly in the case of the small farmer—as opposed to textbook farming consists of making do with what is at hand. And whatever the experts say, farming is not just another industry—it is an occupation, a way of life. Bell described an English peasant-proprietor as

that most honourable, rare and misunderstood of men. It is fineness, not boorishness, that is his hallmark. A feast of English quality it is; his one man's success cancels a host of defects in me, it is the very sweet and secret juice of England that has come to fruition against the bitterest weather, economic and political, of all time.

But alas, since that was written, such men, along with the farm workers, the horses, and the arts of husbandry, have been driven from the land. It was with extraordinary commitment and understanding that Bell prophesied: 'By going back to nature as our educator, we seek to remind ourselves and our fellows of the unchanging laws of our existence. Starve the soil by greed and idleness, take everything out of it and put nothing back, and there follows disease of soil, of plant, of beast and man.' But his words were not heeded.

Like his friends and fellow-writers, H. J. Massingham and C. Henry Warren, he was concerned about the way farming was developing. And in country life he put as much emphasis on rural culture as upon agriculture. He was not, however, as consistent in his attitude to 'scientific farming' as Massingham, and took a more ambivalent view of mechanization. These apparent inconsistencies were the result of his being a farmer and knowing the eternal struggle to beat the weather, to take advantage of the right soil conditions. Machines he thought gave that advantage. He tried to reconcile nature and technology, and *The Flower and the Wheel* was the title of one of his most thoughtful and perceptive books, which Massingham called 'a litany of earth'. That desirable but difficult balance was not achieved; the wheel came to crush the flower, and finally wreck the rural structure, and make the country a landscape without labourers.

One day in 1979 he looked out of his window and wrote, 'Never a ploughman, never a one. In fact one, and only one in a landscape which in my youth was full of horses, men and boys . . . Only the Black Death in the past has so decimated a countryside as modern farming has done.'

In 1939 he moved to Redisham in East Suffolk and there on his farm he bred Red Polls, the Suffolk breed of cattle. In conversation and in his writing he often referred to his favourite cow, Strawberry. And once he wrote a moving account of cattle breeding;

So generation [of cattle] followed generation—in a man's life not so many generations. From the first days of buying some in-calf heifers; just a collection at first (and himself lately married). Then gradually a certain type . . . a certain conformation . . . At last a herd, and not a collection . . . Soon grey hairs are here. What has he achieved? To him it seems nothing, he's no more than begun.

Massingham believed that Adrian Bell was the friend of lords and labourers, saying 'Gold and gems adorn his plough . . . And as he writes in his books so he talks with his friends . . . But if you listen closely to his casual,

INTRODUCTION

rather drawling and desultory words, you inhale poetry as from a bean-field, you perceive truths, you gather wisdom. You think: 'Here is a man who understands the structure of life; how happy am I in his friendship and confidence!'

I knew Adrian Bell for rather more than twenty years and can confirm the accuracy of Massingham's words. Bell, the man, was as good as his books, in fact he was his books and his books were him. I last saw him a few weeks before his death, and even then when he was in great pain he still had something of that incredible youthfulness and quiet sense of humour which he had retained for so long.

And Mrs Bell, she was exactly as you hoped but hardly dared expect to be; in short, the one you are about to meet in *The Cherry Tree*. This book and the succeeding books owe a lot to Mrs Bell. Theirs was indeed a marriage of true minds.

This trilogy is justly famous, and Adrian Bell has been praised as a writer, but I do not believe he has as yet been accorded the honour he undoubtedly deserves. During the latter years of his life it seemed that his work was almost ignored or neglected. Modest as he was, he must have had some idea of his achievement and though he never let it show, this must have been a source of disappointment to him. I can only guess at why he seemed almost forgotten. Perhaps he was hard to place because he belonged to no particular school of rural writing. Perhaps because he used no literary tricks. Perhaps because sensitive and elegant writing were no longer fashionable. I do not know, but I am glad that this trilogy is now available to a new public; and I do know that after many a writer has been forgotten, when many a fashion has died, he will be remembered and his work will still live.

CHAPTER I

How long had I been standing here under the old cherry tree? Minutes or years? While the storm with its batteries of thunder deployed across the sky, letting fall but a few drops—for all its growling—which the boughs above me caught and shook till they sparkled. It was as my man Walter always said; no rain came to us at Silver Ley Farm from the west—that is, from over the murk of trees that were Benfield Manor Park—and if the sky blew up black as ink from there, why, so it might. Walter would be still in his shirt-sleeves, nor even cock an anxious eye.

Although I'd been farming Silver Ley for several years, I was still of little faith in that one respect, and had to pause on my way out to the fields and shelter under the cherry tree against what seemed an imminent cloud-burst. Not that the laughing blossom was any protection, snowing thinly down, but the trunk was curved over like an old man's body, and there was a hollow where once a swarm of bees had hived and the honey had been cut out. Walter remembered that as a boy.

And so, like Christian when he met with Apollyon in the way, my cherry tree brandished its sparkling blossoms at the storm, which drew away muttering, and darting its lightning.

And, like the light of faith justified, the sun shone dazzlingly again on Walter's shirt-sleeves, as he worked with the hoe, and prepared to tell me "I told you so."

But I find myself in memory a long time under the

cherry tree. It was a veteran in a young orchard, standing not many steps from the house, just the spot to which one would resort on fine mornings after breakfast, in that temporary mood of a cigarette, to take stock of the day, and the spot where in summer, coming down hot and thirsty from the harvest-field for that precious quarter-hour of "fourses," one would find tea all ready set out on a white cloth on the grass. There I have watched night take ultimate possession of the earth with a huge sigh in the leaves. I have been among its boughs, too, after the spare fruit, the gay baubles of cherries, when the wind has rocked the tree, and I have felt myself riding the air, rising and falling as with the breath of some cosmic trance.

When I first came to Silver Ley, ruthless as a new broom, I took an axe and felled half an acre of old fruit trees—beautiful things, especially in spring, when, sported with blossoms, their rheumaticky limbs seemed contorted with a kind of bizarre courtesy, a gallant attempt to remember their bow and their curtsey beneath the sprig of youth. But their trunks—yea, even their faintest twigs—were green as grass, and they bore hard, harsh little apples, or none at all, so I had them down despite the entreaty of their attitude, and planted young trees of my favourite sorts in their stead, which was a tacit pledge to myself of many years at Silver Ley to enjoy their fruit.

Only the old cherry tree I spared, who was king of the orchard. My hand had been stayed by Walter's remonstrance in the first place that "that were a master great tree for a cherry, aye, that were the head cherry tree as ever he did see." And so many of his boyhood's pranks had been connected with it, all of which he told me in full detail, that it came to have quite a story for me too, and there was always a ghost of a boy clambering about in it. A bedridden old woman had sent word, or Walter had made out she did, that she hoped I wasn't

6

going to "down" with the old cherry tree, as that made a fine show in the spring, to be seen right from her window in the village, and it did anyone's heart good, especially such as couldn't get about.

I was glad in the spring that it was still there, for it was like a white cloud tethered to earth; its top could be seen billowing up over the horizon from a long way off.

As the years passed, for me too the cherry tree came to be full of associations, so that, as I looked back, the strenuous times were forgotten, and I seemed to have been standing there for a long hour chatting to a now scattered company of strangers, friends, companions, farmers, and men.

But last night we heard a crash above the wind, and this morning the cherry tree is lying at full length along the orchard, having smashed a gap in the hedge with its top, through which the cattle have strayed, and now are rubbing their necks against its topmost branches.

That is why, as I sat down to write this morning, with that great gap of sky where I had expected the familiar boughs alive with bird moments, and found the room more coldly bright, the cherry tree seemed to have been central in all my sunlit hours and the gap of sky a gap in my life also. For, on coming into the room, I had forgotten for the space of a second what had happened. Then, having a number of things concerning my life here to tell of, and going back in thought, seeking where to begin, I saw myself standing under the cherry tree that day in early spring, so I planted it at the head of my page.

CHAPTER II

IT is good to be a bachelor while freedom has still the
bloom on it and is prized for itself alone. I used to pity
those who were married, like men caught in a trap by
one leg; for they never seemed whole-heartedly in one
place, but while with one foot were among a merry
gathering, with the other seemed always stuck fast at
home. They would be ever fingering for their watches,
with mumblings about "the wife expecting me back."
But, after all, the brightest occasion had to finish some
time, even for the freest of us, and I'll admit that the
smile died away as one blundered up the dark garden
path and flashed one's torch on to a mound of white ash
in the living-room grate and the remains of breakfast on
the table. Silence seemed more than silence after late
laughter; and one had no heart to cook a meal, but had
some bread and cheese by an oil stove and went to bed.
At such times I had inklings that perhaps the boot was
on the other leg, and those fellows who always left early
pitied *me*! However that may be, in time mere freedom
became empty of possibility. I wearied of solitude and
married a wife.

(As I am writing a book about a farm I suppose this
last fact should be thus baldly stated and left at that.
But I cannot forbear re-living those disconnected
moments that stand forth in mind as the code by which
memory interprets the past. If anyone is impatient
with me, and would be on the farm, let him go on to
page 19 where I will be with him shortly.)

Now one evening, after I had had my tea, I was rummaging in my cupboard and shuffling my bills when I came upon my first farm account-book, and read again the entries of my early days as a farmer here. That set me musing on the past, and on the year I had spent with Mr. Colville at Farley Hall as a pupil on his farm, then a feckless cockney youth full of baseless fancies. I was very glad the experience had been mine; and, as my evenings were long, lonely, and unoccupied, I began to write of it, the more clearly to summon it up. Yes, after completely renouncing the pen at twenty, at the end of ten years I found myself taking it up again to write, not the mysterious poems of my youth, but a bull-headed account of my year at Farley Hall. It even achieved publication, and that really surprised me, for, though the subject was of interest to me, I didn't think it would be to a world busy for the most part on more novel problems. I enjoyed writing it; it was merely putting on paper the mental diary I had kept of those days, and it somehow made my present life more emphatically worth while. Not that the book, when I received my six gratis copies, seemed to have anything to do with me. I turned the printed pages curiously; and seemed to come face to face with my reflection unexpectedly in a mirror.

One morning I received a letter from one who said she had enjoyed reading of the days at Farley Hall, and the reason for her enjoyment had been, she said, that the life seemed "like clean linen, shining forks and spoons, the beauty of everything you use every day." It was continually with me, as I went about that morning, that such beauty, the bright-worn, manual workaday beauty of what one used, was the light of life for me, though it had not occurred to me in those words. For labour, I feel, is the key to satisfying life, the soother of worry, preparing one also for the appreciation of food and rest. If you consider bodily toil primitive and

9

blunting (as you may be justified in doing), then this beauty is a very pedestrian affair, but I confess I am touched always with a sense of mystery at sight of things that flash and shine with use among the mire they move in; it is always a little miracle of transfiguration—plough-shares, iron toe-pieces of men's boots, fork-prongs, and chains.

There was no address to the letter I received, or I should have written thanking my friend for her words.

Now coincidence, I know, has no story value what-ever; yet every person in actual life experiences one or two startling coincidences, and one of mine was that later I met by chance the person who had written to me.

She lived in London. She worked in an office, in a great block of buildings near the Abbey and facing the hospital at Westminster, whose architecture, supposedly ecclesiastical, actually looked mediæval and prison-like. It looked to me, at all events, like Doubting Castle, in which lived Giant Despair, for how should one single-handed storm that citadel against all the forces and inducements of civilisation, and carry off a woman from its warm imprisonment to the cold freedom of my Anglia? For that was what I intended, having fallen in love.

As I stood at the corner, breasting the storm of traffic, I noticed that a newsvendor had left his pitch tempor-arily; his pile of papers lay on the wall there, held down by a stone: beside it lay a small pile of coppers. As I waited by that building for its prisoner to be let out on parole, I noticed that every so often a passer-by would lift the stone and take a paper, adding also a copper to the pile. Yet, strange to say, no one in this great cyclone of mercenary endeavour thought fit to take those pennies for his own use. This stood as a sign to me that the bark of the city might be worse than its bite.

In fact, this place put into my hand the key which would unlock the door if the prisoner would then walk out into the fields. For quite a number of its citizens had bought my book, and the otherwise impassable gulf of penury was temporarily bridged.

But the future, viewed however optimistically, was a question mark upon a faintly roseate background, which was the Micawber-like hope of something turning up. We—that is, Nora particularly—did not press the matter to the extent of whisking away the pleasant sentiment and exposing the complete blank of ineligibility. And in that, and in a certain weariness of the shoulders after the day's work which it took a glass of sherry under the cosy lamp of the Soho dinner-table to dispel, I first tasted the intoxicating possibility of success. For if I were ineligible with my fifty odd acres, I should have been no less so with five hundred, as any farmer who experienced those times will admit. And those were such times that he who was eligible yesterday might not be so to-morrow; so that mothers knew not what to do for the best.

At least I had little to explain; it was all down in black and white, and she was as familiar with it, she said, as I was.

But sometimes Nora would take a different tone altogether. My courtship (is there a more modern word?) took place over a long series of week-ends. It would be when we had dressed to make an evening of it, Nora in a long daffodil-coloured frock, beringed and coiffured close into the neck—as we dined, with all the evening and its theatre before us, she would suddenly discover some insuperable obstacle which increased my own momentary misgivings that such a vision should ever tread the red-brick floors of Silver Ley.

She had heard, she said, from a friend, that Suffolk possessed the bleakest climate in all England, against which I hastily sought authoritative witness, and memory served up Mr. Prioleau's recommendation of "frozen sunlight."

"Frozen!" Nora shuddered in the warm restaurant.

"But sunlight," I insisted, and pointed out its healthiness compared with the moist and muggy murk of the West Country winter—for my proposal may seem a little less mad if I mention that Nora was really a West Country girl, and only a Londoner of late years through the need of earning a living.

Then she asked, did the bedroom fireplace draw well? As though that might make the climate just possible.

I had to admit there were no fireplaces upstairs— "But a thatched roof," I said hurriedly (it was my only asset), "keeps the cottage very warm in winter and cool in summer."

"Have you a special heater for the water, or is it just the old-fashioned kitchen range affair?"

"Well, in a sense there is a special heater."

"What about the bathroom?"

Again I shook my head.

"What—no bathroom?"

"None," I admitted.

"Then what do you mean about a special heater?"

"I meant the kitchen copper," I said, defensive but defiant, and went on to paint a picture of the drowsy pleasures of sitting in a hip-bath before the glowing kitchen fire—("Like an opened oyster," Nora put in)— with the cat and loudly ticking clock for company. What a delicious resolving of all the ardours of the day that was, as one dabbed oneself nervelessly with soap and water.

But my epicurean flight availed nothing against the sudden crop of doubts which sprang up and seeded themselves a hundredfold in the otherwise barren silence.

Now, indeed, I saw the folly into which love had surprised me. I saw my hopes puffed out with their own breath and tottering on their meagre base. I had written a book which Nora had enjoyed—no more. I had confused life with literature. The person before me was born to be served by magic powers—the flashing leap of electricity, the powerful motions, controlled by a finger pressure, of modern civilisation. Her attitude said so—the poise, the nonchalance. And this is what strikes me about the city-dweller as against the country-man—he may be the slave of his system, in bodily comfort he is a king, and his attitude is always implicit with the knowledge that he has but to lift his finger for any of his reasonable needs to be instantaneously satisfied. He never need exert himself—and therefore, being human, has to "take exercise." But the country-man goes about as though always expecting to have to stoop and grapple with something; he dwells among forces he cannot tame (is that why his windmills look such toys?); and in the spring, with its primrose clouds, he is like Jacob wrestling with an angel.

So then I saw the folly that had led me on to suppose that Nora should exchange her queenship in this glittering hall to stoop beneath my cottage lintel, and that I must grit my teeth and return alone to my fields and their sweetening labours; though not the least of my disappointment was this idyllic evening blighted in the bud.

"I'm sorry it's not good enough for you," I muttered, eyes downcast, but refusing to concede a jot of its goodness to me. But I looked up to find her smiling; and saying gently, "When shall we go there?"

"Where?"

"To Silver Ley."

"But there's no bathroom—nothing."

"Did you think that really mattered to me? Aren't you a booby?" she mocked.

So my heart leaped up again like a lark towering into the dawn, and the future rushed to meet me open-armed.

13

"You and your mother must come down and see the place—soon," I cried.

But she shook her head. "There's no need. I'll take your word for it."

"For the house?"

"For everything."

I gaped. Was ever such a wife? But then I had a flash—"Your mother——"

"She is a practical person."

"And she'd think it——"

"Well," Nora smiled, "you don't expect her to be in love with you too, do you?"

All through the rest of the meal I chattered of the cottage; during the theatre some new detail would keep coming to mind.

"There's a pretty old window between the pantry and the hall," I'd whisper, and a few minutes later, "Do you know anything about gardening? There are two flower-beds in the lawn, and I expect this is the time to be planting things"; until somebody turned round with a demoniacal expression in the half-light and hissed "Sh!"

Memory winnows the past and leaves me with these moments: St. James's Park in late summer sunlight, with a bugle sounding from the barracks and a scarlet regiment marching towards Buckingham Palace—just as though England were a small Ruritanian autocracy, a loud, toylike, military affair—while exotic waterfowl disported themselves in the lake, and banks of dahlias rivalled the soldiery for colour.

A day in Richmond Park, when we sat so still that two deer came leaping past us unwitting of our presence. . . .

A day in latest autumn in Kew Gardens, with the air cold as contrition after the foliage-framed vistas (as of a Victorian chapter-heading) of the hot-houses, and a mantle of leaves in the deserted walks, and here and there a stooping, unsuspected gardener, and a tree with boughs drooping over, as though to pick up again the leaves it had let fall; all still and strange as a dream through which we walked together. . . .

A day in which I went with a ring for Nora—a ring sold me by a pretty Irish assistant, who, being engaged herself, exercised a sweet discrimination—a sunny day, and me, of course, with much time to spare for the appointment, so that I walked across St. James's Park to waste some of it, and there found my way barred by a concourse and police and military lining the way in readiness for the King's setting forth to open Parliament —a fact which had entirely escaped my mind. So that when the fanfare sounded, and the bewigged couriers and outriders came by, it was getting so late that I was almost put to it to beg a lift of His Majesty in his gilt and crystal coach, which, my errand being such, he might not have refused me had he known my emergency, and his equipage "passing the door," as they say, on its route.

Police seemed to head me off in every direction except that in which I had come; but I arrived at my destination on the tick after all, as undignified as a bolted rabbit, and had the pleasure of waiting five minutes for milady, which enabled me to get my breath.

So, somehow, to acceptance and approval in the parental home; though I am still hazy as to how we brought this about—I blundering in the traditional suitor fashion, I know; Nora, most assured, making great play with the thatched roof ("warm in winter, cool in summer") about which she had seemed so unconvinced, backing it up with information all of her own about "modern odourless oil stoves."

At any rate, I remember three brimming wine-glasses like three red tulips under the light, touching together and rising to three pairs of lips in honour of the compact of that day.

Then to get married; not so easy as it sounds. One reads of those impulsive marriages (almost) at first sight, and striking while the iron is hot on the anvil of Gretna Green. Immediate marriage is for the rich (I cannot think why, as impatience is evenly distributed among the classes), while for the average citizen what rusty wheels of ancientry must be set creeping round, while he fumes like a mettlesome horse halted on the very brink of his leap over into the promised land. Life stood still, and Time seemed to, while we debated church or register office; the latter seemed the more honest for us, but, after half a day of seeking, it turned out to be a dingy villa with cracked window-sills, approached by a garden of black and drooping remains of flowers. A terrier rushed at us with hysterical fury when we rang the bell, and shouts for "Ma!" resounded within. Ma opened to us, revealing age-yellow paper on the passage wall; we had both no other idea than escape by then, but Ma fastened on us with expectations of her husband's immediate return, and, that failing, tried to pin us down to a definite call on the morrow with an anxiety that in this world means but one thing—the expectation of money. So we were "customers," young couples being sold into bondage on the premises. It was all quite impossible, this cracked relic of a street with the trams clanging by at the end of it, and we went to see the verger of the big church in the square. In a draped sitting-room so near the church that the hush of it leaked in somehow, the verger presented us with the "price-list," so to speak. Choir-boys, as I remember, were a shilling each. Bells, I think, were a guinea.

My marriage morn. The brooding height and space of the church afflicted me again with the unnameable terror that a church always held for me as a child. There I stood with the shiftings, the coughs, of the invited and uninvited going on behind me, and the busy tap-tap-tap of the verger's feet sounding staccato, with pauses, like a code message. I faced a flaming east window, thankful that I hadn't also to face rows of choir-boys at a shilling apiece, for I should have felt like an employer of sweated labour. I felt, amid all these little rustlings, like Bishop Hatto listening to the invasion of the rats into his tower. The gilded eagle spread his wings near by with a glorious freedom I couldn't emulate. My best man, who was a bit of a sportsman, whispered in my ear, "Cock pheasant coming over!"

But Nora came, and then it was soon over—the being likened to Isaac and Rebecca, the being joined hand to hand when we were already joined more securely heart to heart, the being prayed over at the altar with all one's consciousness perforce in one's knees, that groaned aloud on the marble, and the sudden voice and un-expected presence of the verger in the choir-stalls intoning responses. For some reason we chose, of all months, January in which to be married, largely because warmer times were so many months away, and Nora thought it best to get the worst over first. As a matter of fact, I think she didn't trust my handling of the flower-beds, and she was determined on having a pretty garden for the summer.

I had left many instructions with the wife of my man Walter. For, after my accounts of Silver Ley to Nora, I had had private misgivings—was it really as good as all that? I wanted it to look as bright as Nora's trust in it, even in January, that she should not be disappointed at first sight of her home. For this I shall ever be grateful to Mrs. Walter, who had a blaze of logs in the living-room, and the kettle puffing, and the tea all set out, with bread of her own baking and cakes of her own making; and her cheerful self, broad and apronly, to bustle us in out of the bitter twilight.

Nora exclaimed with pleasure, and I too saw it with new eyes. Even the makeshift bachelor furniture seemed composed and at one in the harmony of beams and firelight.

And Mrs. Walter had culled from some sequestered corner a handful of flowers—snowdrops, aconites, three different coloured primulas, and two violets, and stood them in a glass in the centre of the tea-table.

CHAPTER III

ABOUT a week after we had started married life at Silver
Ley the sky became leaden with vague menace, and
Walter, who had been predicting snow for several days,
was justified. Country people seem to have a greater
prescience of snow than of any other kind of weather,
foretelling it even before its grey shadow overcasts the
earth.

I had grown used to a powder-bowl on my dressing-
table, but still not to the poetry of woman's, as against
the prose of man's, attire. Most of the day it would
be athletic wool and tweed; but when I came in at tea-
time I'd find a transformation had taken place; Nora
would be sitting in a sensitive silken frock, with earrings
like two drops of dew in the lamplight, in the room she
had re-arranged. It was as though she had sat there all
day, like a bird in its nest; it was full of the sense of
repose.

Before coming in I had noticed a fire by my boundary
hedge, and wondered what was the cause of it, as neither
Walter nor I had been hedging there, and I didn't suppose my neighbour had gone mad and begun cutting my
hedge for me.

Tea-time is best as then, when it coincides with the
hour that ends in darkness. I looked out at stars and
snow and saw the fire plainly now, flickering up from
behind the hedge. So I went out, for curiosity's sake,
to investigate. The stars were very bright, and a crescent
moon lay on its back with a brilliant star almost in its

arms, low over Benfield church tower like the banner
of Islam advanced upon the citadel of Christendom,
which in other days might have been taken for a portent.

But the ruddier flame led me over the sheet of the snow
with its mysterious script of minute happenings. I came
to the hedge and looked over, and there saw a gipsy
woman and seven children sitting round the fire. The
woman was huddled in shapeless wrappings like a Red
Indian squaw. She smoked a short clay pipe upside
down. The children were wild-haired and half-naked,
with coal-black shining eyes. They all sat on their
haunches as still as statues, except for the children's hair
which blew in the wind, in a complete circle round this
core of fire in the deathly waste of snow. All their eyes
brooded on it, drinking the flame into them, except for
the woman's, which were slumbrous and wrinkled at
the corners. She seemed to drowse over it in a state of
fulfilment, an empty, fire-blackened tin at her side.
She was steeped in a kind of sullen sufficiency; as
though for the moment her maternity gave her rest,
her sevenfold increase being satisfied with food and
warmth. She sat dozing with her pipe. But a dwind-
ling flame knit her brows with deeper shadow, added a
resentfulness that acknowledged Time to be her taskmaster. She looked like a symbol to me in the vast and
glittering night, a dark, uncouth reality to which the
stars were as tinsel; turning her back on the waste of
death about her, hoarding this one red bud of life; the
strong, wry root of which Nora and our tea-hour were
the flower. The strangeness of it was to find us neighbouring so close to cowering need after all, against
which the light-hearted pattern on our cups and plates
screened us with illusion, and all our poetry about the
stars.

It was hardly dawn when I heard, half-awake, their
caravan creak by under our window. I returned to the
spot in the morning, for it seemed like a dream, but there

were the ashes of the fire and innumerable imprints of small, bare feet in the snow.

There's not much you can do on a farm in the snow. The fields are all strange and glaring with a sterile purity; it is like a second flood, with the steep-roofed barn, from which the first glance of sunlight sends the snow slithering in soft cascades, an ark adrift on the monotonous waste. We on the farm were besieged by the weather—the chickens huddled in the cart-shed, the pigs stayed in their sleeping-quarters, the cows were not let out after milking, but stood in the yards all day, ruminating and steaming. The men, too, were confined to the buildings, doing odd jobs, mending things that were broken—unless a sortie were made with horse and cart to the root-clamp to get a good supply into the barn against fine days when all would be busy on the land. Those were mornings on which everything the men moved shed first a white replica of itself on the snow.

I had bought a great cask, which, halved, would replace the two swill-tubs in which the pigs' food was mixed, as these leaked badly. I set Walter and a man I had working for me at the time to sawing this cask in two. For a while I heard the saw moving rhythmically. Then it grew irregular, with many stops and starts and long silences in between. At last the attempts to set the saw going seemed so unavailing that it never sounded twice before ceasing again. I stopped what I was doing and went over to find out what impeded them in so simple a piece of work. As I crossed the yard I was surprised to hear a burst of song from the barn. It was Walter's voice—Walter, the most reserved of men— rich, reckless and full-throated. Had the snow surprised him into a carol? Nothing of the sort. As I came nearer I heard him roaring that "every night" there were "robberies in the park," and in consequence he was "afraid to go home in the dark"—this last with a bravado singularly unsuited to the words.

I opened the barn-door and found one man collapsed into a cave of chaff with a grin of speechless imbecility, while Walter was enthroned on a heap of roots with a mangold poised in his palm like a royal orb. This he playfully threw at my head as I entered. The energy of the movement caused a subsidence in the pile of globes which sent Walter rolling on to the floor in roars of laughter.

The atmosphere reeked of wine—of port—which emanated from the partially sawn-through cask, as I found out when I stooped over it. I sniffed into it, and soon began to discover the reason of Walter's riotous behaviour, for the odour was so strong that it caused a gradual melting of care in the core of my being; and persuaded my lips into a smile. Walter and I exchanged the broadest of grins, while I discovered I was glad of the support of the tub and wondered why the rafters of the barn had become so unsteady.

Then I heard Nora calling my name. "All righ', all righ'; coming," I muttered, and stumbled across the scattered mangolds—not the easiest of obstacles to weak legs—and got out into the snow-cold air again. Nora met me to say that a man had called to see me; but my face had become quite uncontrollable, a kind of helpless beatitude kept mounting and mounting in my heart and I felt myself grinning from ear to ear. Nora's face suddenly blanched, and she said in a small voice of horror, "You're drunk."

"Drunk!" I cried, with an elaborate gesture of denial. "I haven't touched a drop"—which was literally true: I lurched past her to the man who was standing in the yard and shook him heartily by the hand. He, too, seemed very pleased to meet me, for he was a traveller in veterinary stuffs, and after an introductory yarn or two managed to sell me an absurd quantity of blood salts for cattle. I'm sure I was his easiest customer that day. As he drove away the cold air was beginning to counteract the fumes from the cask, and I beginning to doubt the apparently irrefutable argument that it was an economy to buy in bulk. Even if constipation were chronic in cows, which for the part of my three was far from the case, I estimated that I had enough of this remedy to last them a year or more.

Nora faced me indoors with a tear starting from each eye. I plunged my head in cold water and was myself again. Then I explained what had happened and how we had been overpowered by the fumes of wine imprisoned in the empty cask. It was now dinner-time, and, to prepare Walter's wife for his arrival, I went over to her cottage. "I'm afraid your husband's slightly intoxicated," I told her.

She was furious. "How dare you say such a thing? I've been married to him this twenty year and he ain't come home drunk once. Walter 'toxicated? Why, he ain't had a drop this week."

"Neither has he to-day," I began, but at that moment Walter rolled in, flung his cap into a corner, and flopped into a chair.

"Well, that's a rum 'un," ejaculated his wife, and Walter echoed dazedly, with distant eyes, "That do be a rum 'un, and no mistake."

I explained to her the cause, and left her still wondering, but vastly relieved, and inclined herself to see the joke.

Some may doubt the possibility of one becoming intoxicated on the mere odour of wine, but I assure them that that cask grinned causeless joviality at us through its split side, and I recommend the purchase of one like it to any scrupulous persons who have signed the pledge and regret them of it. For a pledge is a pledge—but there is no obligation that the smell of drink should be avoided. It may not always work, of course, for as our local doctor said when I told him of the matter, "That's good health. It doesn't take much to intoxicate a healthy man as a rule, but if a person living on his nerves had walked in there he probably wouldn't have turned a hair." And he told me how once he had been becalmed in a small yacht and was without anything except a bottle of whisky, and in a short time had drunk the whole quantity neat and merely felt sustained.

"March brings breezes loud and shrill." It brought also legal troubles for me. The other person working for me at this time besides Walter I have referred to as a "man": I miscalled him in so doing. He was one of those baffling creatures with the head of a man and the body of a boy who are loosely termed "village idiots." He was certainly half-witted, but there was about him the air that the other half of his wits were somewhere else rather than non-existent. He used to wrinkle his deep-sunk eyes and stare at me or the thing in his hand as though it were a long way off, or a writing hard to decipher. He had never quite mastered the language of common things—shape did not suggest use to him. For instance, he would be sent by Nora to fetch coal, and take a bucket in each hand. Sometimes he'd be away about ten minutes and return with the buckets as empty as before. He'd stand in the threshold staring at them and at her vacantly and apologetically, having completely forgotten what he had been sent to do. The sight of a bird's shadow passing over the ground was enough to cause a gap of surprise in his mind, and then he would have to return and be told his errand again. The second time he usually accomplished it. He sounds exasperating, but Nora, with that imperious largesse of spirit which makes a queen of any who bestows it, was gentle and pleasant with him, never chided him for the shadows that fell across his path, and gave him a cup of cocoa and a slice of cake every morning at eleven. The result was that he became as devoted to her as a dog, for I think she was the first person who had ever shown him kindness; the villagers mocked him, and at home he was told to make himself scarce by a shrew of a mother and a father who was embittered against the world by failure at keeping a public-house. Often, I think, he slept in our barn among the hay, for he used to arrive in the morning with bits of it in his hair like a Shakespearian clown.

Though he would miss the meaning of a pail on occasion, he had a keen eye for the corners where Nature achieved her small perfections. In the spring he would bring in birds' eggs—large and small, of many lovely hues. He seemed to measure the value of each by the prowess necessary to its capture. Once, walking through a wood, I was greatly startled to discover him clambering about in the boughs above me. Mornings and evenings, before and after work, he would be found in the most impossible places, and I consulted with Nora as to how we could deflect his ardour into some safer expression, and one which involved less sacrifice of wild life—for they were by no means common eggs which he brought in, many of them. Nora transferred his interest to the gathering of wild flowers, of which he brought in a variety unsuspected by me, from the fields that I worked in all day. This was improved on by giving him a small patch of the garden in which to plant them by the roots, and we soon had quite a remarkable collection of the farm's flora in those few square feet.

Of course, I only paid Billy (that was his name) about half a man's wage. Technically his job was what is locally called (spelt phonetically) "Bacchus boy." Not that he was our Ganymede, nor had the name any connection with the effects of the wine-cask, but was a contraction of the term "back-house" boy, because his work was the doing of odd jobs about the buildings at the back of the house. Most farm-labourers start as that.

Later, his father managed to scrape enough together to set up as a horse-dealer, and passing Silver Ley in the spring, would see his son often doing work in the fields—hoeing, or helping with the corn-drilling. Being a suspicious person, he formed the idea that I was profiting by his son's simplicity, and, while engaging him as a back-door loon, was using him for a man's work in the fields. So he came to me with the news that his son had been twenty-one for the best part of a year, and what was I going to do about it? I said, no more than I had been doing, and that he should be thankful to have his son employed at all and kept out of mischief. He was welcome, I said, to find the farmer who would employ him at more than I gave him.

The man became enraged, and said we'd see about that, and he'd bring it before the Wages Board. I too became angry, and asked if he suggested I was taking advantage of his son. He replied that, like most farmers, I knew which side my bread was buttered, etc., etc. As a result, I vowed I'd cease to employ the boy if he made a legal case of it. He did, and my case was upheld, but, owing to my having omitted to obtain a legal exemption, I was liable for the full wages payable to a man of twenty-one since Billy's birthday.

So Billy was sacrificed to the senseless quarrel. Actually, I think his father wanted him, and merely saw his way to extorting money from me by these tactics. He used him to fetch his horses home. When he had bought a horse, he would set Billy on its back and drive comfortably away himself in his gig. Often since he left us Nora and I have passed Billy riding bare-back some rusty-looking purchase of his father's, a hunched, swaying figure, sometimes as much as twenty miles away from home, with darkness fallen long ago, and snow in the wind.

Troubles of a kind never come singly, and it was not long after I had faced the Wages Board Committee that the policeman came to enquire, had I a dog licence for the black retriever lolling at my gate, now obviously more than six months old? I understood a farmer was allowed to keep a dog without a licence, I replied. But here again I had omitted that increasingly essential thing in modern life—an official permit. The policeman was sorry—had he known he would have warned me before, being a friendly policeman, and an ally of the farmers against gipsies, tramps, and other roaming persons. But it was too late now; the authorities were already on my track, and I should have to answer a summons.

The law is impartial, not only in its judgments, but in the tone of its arraignments. The man who has forgotten to get a seven-and-sixpenny dog-licence is called on to answer for himself with the same stern resonance as is the murderer.

"The Bench" sat all along one side of a long table on a dais, with, in their midst, a Jehovah-like gentleman whose great beard made his mouth look very dark and deep and awful when he opened it to speak.

I was summoned to the dock, where I stood while the clerk read out the accusation. Then I was commanded to plead. I could but murmur "Guilty." Then our friendly policeman was summoned to the witness-box, where he laid his helmet aside, took up the Bible, and swore upon it to tell the truth, the whole truth, and nothing but the truth—so help him, God.

He went on to relate how he had come to my farm, had seen the dog, had asked me as to a licence, etc., all in a cold metallic tone quite other than that actually employed on the occasion. What, had he forgotten the glass of beer, and how he had asked me did I think that

27

poultry spice really paid for giving to laying hens?
Had he forgotten our mutual suspicions about old
Gomper's rick-fire—and our harmonious political
views? "Et tu, Brute?"

HAD I ANYTHING TO SAY? Jehovah of the Bench
demanded. I spoke in apologetic extenuation, and
was fined ten shillings.

Following mine was another dog-licence case—a
labourer with a face resigned to troubles. He faced the
magistrates with defeated eyes. He had six children
and earned twenty-eight shillings a week. He couldn't
afford the money for the licence. He had been saving
up for it, but he couldn't afford it yet.

"What, you have a wife and six children to keep on
twenty-eight shillings a week, and you keep a dog?
You've no business to—it's disgraceful," thundered
Jehovah.

"Well, you see, sir, the little dog—it's a fox-terrier
dog, well, sort of white terrier dog——"

"The breed and size is immaterial," Jehovah said.

"Well, sir, the dog was give to my youngest girl as a
pup, and the kids got that fond of it, I didn't like to do
away with it when it come to be six months old."

"You should have had it destroyed if you couldn't
afford a licence."

"But the kids had taught it to do tricks and that, and
it would have fair upset them if I'd had to kill it."

"You should never have allowed them to have a
dog to get fond of. Do you realise that you're a very
improvident man?"

The fine was ten shillings.

"But I can't pay ten shillings," said the man, grasping
the front of the dock.

"Then you'll have to go to prison."

"How can I pay ten shillings on twenty-eight shillings
a week, and six children?" he asked with desperate
rhetoric.

"You should have thought of that before," was all that the bearded one could say, while the others, made uneasy by the way in which the law had pinned the man in a corner, presented faces like blank walls, deafly, sightlessly, stonily defending themselves.

But the man gave no quarter. "How can I pay ten shillings on twenty-eight shillings a week?" he insisted. "You know I haven't got ten shillings."

His eyes searched them, but none looked at him and the unanswerable problem of his penury. They became Pilates, washing their hands of this man, of the death of his dog, of the tears of his children. They had citadels of their own to defend against the world's ravage.

"Then I'll have to go to prison," he said with finality, without fear, having come to the last wall of his defence.

"You can pay if you have time. We'll allow you three weeks in which to pay."

"I can't pay," the man said stubbornly. "I'll go to prison."

"Three weeks in which to pay," Jehovah said, pretending not to hear.

"I'll go to prison."

But the clerk rose, and in the gentle tone of a mediator said that the man's fine had been paid. The Bench relaxed their fixity—one slackened his shoulders, another coughed, a third lifted his head.

For momentarily I had become a Socialist and required no change from my pound note. Had I not seen Jehovah in a closed car, smoking a cigar?

I answered the clerk's questioning brow with a gesture coupling the man in the dock with the ten shillings change being offered me, and immediately made my escape.

I escaped into sunlight and a wind like soft laughter, out of the squalid little manufacturing town into the fields of bare earth waiting upon spring. Ah, but

THE CHERRY TREE

what a day it is, that day in March which redeems the
land from winter. When the fields say, "We are ready,"
and you leave the plough to stand with the half-turned
furrow drying into a brick upon its breast. Yes, you
leave the plough and its stiff journey, and take the
harrows—first the heavy harrows that hustle the clods
apart, that give them no rest, shouldering them this
way and that till they break and crumble. Then I
took the light harrows that rest so gently upon the
level field, and hitched on to them my chestnut horse,
Darkie. They floated along, tinkling against one
another, their short, straight teeth rippling through
the tilth as fingers through the current of a river. The
plough cuts the earth like a prow forcing its way, but
the light harrows move like a raft riding the surface.

There were few flowers yet, and the trees and hedges
were bare, but this was, and always will be for me,
the very spring, when the clog of winter mud becomes
a dry sift which one treads softly like a carpet, and the
horse treads with ease, pulling the light harrows. Their
short teeth fondle and tease the earth as though for
pleasure at its new fineness, like the pleasure of fingers
in running water, and the only sound is the tinkling
of the chains and the song of a lark poised above, a
black flickering day-star of life.

I followed the harrows all that afternoon, wearing
them back from a winter of rust—(all winter they had
hung on the roof of a straw-stack to keep the straw
from blowing away)—back to the silver gleam of use,
wearing away also the taste of the town where men
sit in judgment on one another, and the estranging
folly of "Socialism," "anti-Socialism," and all hardening
of the heart into attitudes, till I breathed again the
beauty of freedom in obeying the summons of the earth
and the sun, and was as light in heart as the soil I trod.

CHAPTER IV

THERE could have been no less propitious time at which to start, no time when it was more difficult to summon the buoyancy of hope with which it is necessary and natural that two people should start—if the initial mood is to determine whether they discover life together or merely endure it.

Whether economic depression stares more gauntly at you in town or country I do not know. Whether dusty, empty shops are worse than roofless barns. At least Nature is very quick to smooth over man's failures with her moss and creepers; but a street of empty shops is like a sightless man.

Certainly it was a time unparalleled—even the old men admitted as much, which was an unheard-of concession. What was more, the elderly farmers ceased even their murmurs about their sons, that young men didn't know what work meant nowadays, etc. With tennis lawns grown lank and unlevel, drives green and houses patchy, hedges high, yards empty, it was all too plain that their sons did know what work meant, as labour had to be cut to such a minimum that it was ceaseless toil for them.

For they, the young men, would kindle at a word, being desperate with work and ever trying of something new to make it show a profit—and flash back at their elders the latest low record of market prices. In fact, I remember in the Cock Inn one day, where many stopped on the way home from market, hearing old

Will Russet—who had divided his land among his three sons and retired to a house in the village—harking back to the days when three pounds of pork could be bought for a shilling. Whereat his youngest son, who had just entered, ripped off the paper from a parcel he was carrying and thrust a joint of bacon under his father's nose with, "There, two and ninepence I gave for that; that's at the rate of fourpence a pound—so you can guess what sort of price the pigs I sent to market made to-day."

Later came days when the shops of the market towns displayed notices offering twenty-eight shillings' worth of goods for a golden sovereign, and many a cottager's hoard buried under a floor-brick saw the light. These were days when "dole" days at those towns occasioned as much traffic on the roads leading to them as market days. The contradiction of industrial enterprise and atrophy used to stare at each other across the street in the strangest ways. In one little town, while its market threatened to dwindle away through lack of farmers with any stock to send to it, the march of civilisation was symbolised by pylons striding gigantically over hill and dale to its very doors. Premises were taken in its one street and an electrical showroom opened, whose central attraction was a great oxidised silver fire-basket of the baronial sort filled with a warm glow of make-believe coals, while outside the wind cut along the pinched little thoroughfare, of which the only population seemed to be the knot of unemployed whose gathering-place happened to be just opposite. They stood gazing apathetically across at the luxurious appliance which winked ruddily back at them, while, in between, the plate-glass window was like that invisible barrier which starves the world in the midst of its plenty.

They wore a look, those men, which reminded one sharply of the war. One last saw it *en masse* in the faces and attitudes of soldiers about to return to the front. It was the expression of those who have nothing to live for.

Sometimes one met them walking about the country lanes, fecklessly, in the *ennui* of an eternal Sunday. Once, particularly, I was struck by a contrast. For on in front of me went a group of these lads, whose every gesture, even seen from behind, bespoke a lethargic disrelation with their surroundings. They walked each as though his hinder foot did not know why it was being summoned to take another single pace onward, so that they lurched to the side and seemed always to be colliding with one another as they walked, this row of six, like jolted bottles, and vainly their eyes sought the hedge, the trees, for anything to catch their interest. Occasionally they guffawed; one would begin a song on an impulse which wouldn't last till he might finish it, and all the while they whipped their legs idly with green wands they had pulled from the hedge.

Striding from the opposite direction I observed a man, old but not bent, bearded and buskined. He carried a stick—not the limp plaything of the youths, but an ash-pole, shoulder-high. He grasped this near the top, and planted it firmly before him at every other step. His steps were straight, neither hurried nor loitering, but continuing regularly. He gazed only in the direction he was going. He silently saluted me with a motion of his head as he passed. His face had that stern and steady look of the old but not senile; his eyes saw only his destination, but they were eyes that had absorbed their surroundings—he could have told me whether the oak or the ash were the more forward, or when the hedge beside us had been cut last, or which way the clouds were moving. He was a purposeful part of the place he walked in. The youths he passed were as foreign to it as the tarmac on the road, walking in that light daze of the drug of indolence, swaying with its dull intoxication. They stared aside at him, began to titter. But he passed them as though they were not, and they ceased. I was struck by this crossing of the paths of the old man who had a destination and the youths who had none. For it seemed to me that the zest of life had died from them, while it had not yet forsaken a man of seventy odd years.

For the agricultural labourer there were no half-measures. If he were employed, he was comparatively well off, for at thirty shillings a week, with a large garden and a cottage rent of a shilling or two, if anything, a man can get along pretty well—for when bacon was last at fourpence a pound his wages were about twelve shillings. If unemployed, he had sharply to shift for himself and get into town and qualify for the dole, or on to the roads if he were lucky, for his cottage would very soon fall down over his head, seeing that the farmer could hardly keep repaired the cottages of his employees, certainly no others.

It was the farmer who floundered, stuck fast in the mire of debt till he could go neither forward nor back. Joe Boxted, for instance, our neighbour on the one hand, a big man bursting out of the shoulders of his jacket; he had bought his hundred acres on the encouragement of the Corn Production Act in 1920, and now he stood on the solitary cornstack his lone strength had been able to gather from Time's gradual invasion of his land with grass, amid his ruined buildings, with two of the hungriest sows in the county rattling and gnawing their hurdles, a horse like Don Quixote's, and a single, lovely, gentle Alderney cow for whose well-being he would starve the whole farm, his wife and himself.

He was like a bull at bay: the darts of officialdom shot home till he was savage with them. He would be scratching his head to think how he could muster a few pounds to buy some seed corn when a notice of distraint for tithe would be served on him, or a demand for land tax.

He would flourish his pitchfork at me on those occasions as though it were I who was making the demand, and swear he'd hang for murder rather than pay. Once the tithe-owners arranged an auction sale of his goods, but on the day appointed he had managed to gather such a dangerous-looking crowd from all parts of the locality that the auctioneer, seeing them and the proximity of a green pond in the same glance, hastily re-entered his car, saying that the sale was postponed, and drove off.

Joe's cow was the most coveted of his goods, and there came to be quite a rivalry between the different claimants as to which could carry her off to be sold for the money due. But I really think Joe would have defended her with his life. As it was, he always contrived to have his cow somewhere else when his unwelcome callers appeared, and all they got was curses. She'd gone to the bull, that was all he'd tell them: she became as elusive as a will-o'-the-wisp.

Once I found her in a retired paddock of mine, and I informed Joe, who said he was sorry she'd strayed there. But as he came to drive her home in the dusk we exchanged a smile of understanding, for one couldn't but sympathise with surly Joe and his love for that jewel of a creature. It had been his cherished intention to found a fine herd with her, but when it came to the point he used to get such good and persistent bids for her calves at times when the money was so very handy that he'd had to sell them. Her, however, he would not sell, come the four corners of the world in arms—and she was still the whole of his herd.

Sometimes she was found to have "strayed" into one of my other neighbours' meadows. But they all let her stay until Joe came round scratching his head and asking with a fine show of bewilderment, "Have you seen anything of my Daisy?" as though he had been looking everywhere for her.

It had died away—the old bluff, hospitable life of the countryside—like a summer's day. I saw it fade, not as part of it, but from the top of my stacks as I worked, or from the window of my barn. For the economic depression had caused me to hang up my hunting-crop early, and, except for occasional afternoons alone beside my own hedges, my gun. It died slowly, like a cloudless afternoon, splendid to the last. Fewer grew the company that followed the hounds over the fields. Memory contracts the years, and I see the pink coats in successive waves through the meadows and up the hill, and always they seem to melt and melt before the unseen enemy, until sometimes it appears as if only the few leaders remain. In those days the chasing of the fox through the dilapidated country—the spruce rich-red fox—came to seem as anomalous as tilting at windmills.

But they never gave up—often one might see them trotting by one's windows in the morning with the prospects and strategy of the chase still the keen reality in their eyes, though their brows grew ever a shade darker with care, as one after another mammoth poultry-house with its attendant wiring came to stand in fields of rough grass that lately had been under the plough. For the chicken and the fox represent two fundamentally opposed interests.

The country round us became lonely, thinly populated. The old community I had known on coming here ten years ago or more was now almost all gone. But while I—while we—could continue to live here we should stay. Perhaps to see the return of good times and another hopeful generation come to take up their

abode in and about the deserted farmsteads, to rebuild
and repair, to make spruce the lawns, the hedges, and
re-gravel the drives. Or perhaps to see our parlous
world collapse, with the nations rending one another
in the economic pit that each had dug at the door of
his neighbour. But, even then, one day these things
would have to be rebuilt, repaired, for ultimately the
earth is our only sustenance.

It was well to remember that, sitting under one's
cherry tree, in the fey-woven seat of its twisted roots,
sifting the real from the unreal in an uncertain time.
To watch—to watch long and begin to apprehend the
intricate mechanisms of Nature, into which she has
blown the breath of life. To teach one's body to stoop
again to the earth, to use the plough and the scythe,
and feel the balance of their shapes, and seek if one
might discover, in an age that makes a heaven of
labour-saving, why toil was not banished out of Eden.
To observe the starry faith of the blackthorn twig in
spring to come (like one that listens to the ground and
hears a far approach), and resolve upon one's own true
wish in life.

Money-lust, luxury-lust, and the other ingredients
of ambition fail one late or soon. Surely it were better,
rather than serve a life-sentence to the machine of
modern scuffle, to live in a hole in a rock on lentil
porridge, that one might save one's soul alive in looking
at the view. Since life offers no second chances, the
adventure of a morning's walk over familiar fields is not
lightly to be forgone.

The modern consciousness appears to me meteoric
with the impetus of many generations, but glancing,
fitful, like a flame that feverishly gutters. I, too, have
felt myself the child of those centuries, and the tyranny
of the too-inward mind, as lost as free, and sought the
salvation of toil, calming, clarifying, evaporating the
fume of moods, till faith should form itself. Without

the pole-star of a new simplicity, it seems to me, civilisation will continue by turns at deadlock or mad speed, like a machine out of control which bumps itself from one obstacle to another until it falls to pieces.

At any rate, such considerations led us here, to live on little, but at least to live. For, as an advertisement said the other day, "Half a man's life is spent in and around his office." Of the rest he must sleep another half; so is it not a sad thing to be married and have only a quarter of your life in which to enjoy your woman's company? Rather would we sit at the still roots of life, sometimes to talk, sometimes to be silent; to awake and have joy in the rush of the wind, or again to be tired and sit round the fire, and take a book from the shelf put near in preparedness for that evening hour when to do more than reach a hand for it were too much. Such days are long, but eternity were too short for the richness of a double vision.

My former gruff, country-bachelor life had been like a rough crust of bread torn with the hands. Then came Nora, to suspend of a sudden my careless foot, to kneel beneath the old cherry tree and part the grass with her fingers, revealing to me the first primrose of our young year. Then it was I saw the change and the more than compensation, even as my foot was suspended over the wan flower; saw all that callow eagerness had carelessly trampled these many years; saw that, little hurried as my life had been, it had yet been on occasion too hurried, and close as my gaze had been about me, it had yet not been close enough. No, not that alone, but the quality of my application also. One misses the flower when one is watching the bank, fingering a trigger.

This, then, was the siren, disguised as four tender petals, the mystery that puzzled the bachelors gay—

how so-and-so had changed for so-much-the-duller, the disinclined-to-roam, since he became married. Ah, but the flower owed its miracle to the hand that discovered it to me, and its power to turn my foot aside.

CHAPTER V

THERE were spheres of influence. Nora's the cottage,
which was now like a lustre, all polished surfaces and
rippling grains of wood; the tranquil, eddying flow of
life through years from the bursting of a seed. Under
the shine of our long oak table a lost century ebbed
softly away for ever. . . .

Mine the farm. A change here too. Year by year
the choppy sea of ploughland was being superseded by
grass. A green sameness, which was like a stillness
after the various earthen geometry of the plough,
possessed the place. The gnarled stumps of hedges,
close-chopped every year and writhing all ways as in
an agonised attempt to escape the knife, were allowed
to grow, and arose into grace, and dangled bryony
and wild-rose wreaths, and were close-knit into paddock
walls by a gentler art than that which merely kept
them down so that they should not shade the corn at
harvest. Gradually I laid it down to grass—a few
acres a year, for it is expensive to set land down to
grass—and increased my stock. Not but that I missed
all the various moods of the soil through the arable
year with which I had grown accustomed—the uncouth
bareness of winter, the level brown blank of the field
harrowed and drilled on the eve of spring, in which the
late sun surprises depths of hue undreamed of at noon.
And then, when the flame of life catches it, and all
in a night and a day, it seems, it becomes a vivid sheet
of green corn-blades trembling as with eagerness to

get higher, higher—reaching for the sun. Barley is
the blade of spring, the most joyous, for it does a little
pirouette; it goes up with a flourish, a twist, which
makes the whole expanse delicate, like a green haze.
Then, all of a sudden, it tires; its rising blades weary of
their own weight and bow over to the earth again like
a fountain. As for the wheat, after its first uprush in
the waning year the cold smites it. All winter it shivers
like a starveling child, and when the sun grows kind
again it is more cautious; instead of rising up as before,
it first spreads its roots to grapple the earth more surely,
and its green shoots lay themselves close to the ground
and grow along it for quite a way before it dares again
to rise. But soon the blades fall back accomplished,
and from their heart arises the stalk, more vulnerable,
but firmer, being not all complaisance to the wind, but
bending a little, and resisting a little with the strength
of its body. For its upthrust is not any more a mere
dance of joy in being alive above the ground, but a
mission, a purpose—the flower and the seed. Now its
colour deepens to a sober green. Now, hooded and
sheathed like something rare, the ear rises. The stalk
braces itself, and proudly, carefully, slowly lifts the ear
to the greatest height it can, that it may receive the whole
of the light. There the ear unveils itself, and takes
the air, and nods and sways above its abashed, retiring
blades. And now, as the ears appear, the cornfield
receives a voice, and seems to whisper to itself all day
of the majesty of the ear. And now the barley-field
shines like silk with its bearded heads, and all the corn-
lands move like a sea and make visible the breathing of
the wind as it pulses over them. And while the fields
are this great murmurous concourse, they change
their colour, to gold of several shades the wheat, and
the barley blanched "white unto harvest." Oats have
a separate dance of their own of every grain upon its
little wire, and a separate intricate game with the sun-

light in the miniature tree of its ear, catching it and losing it as spray does.

Now the stalks grow stiff and sapless like old men, and can no more bend and play with the wind, but can only stand offering up their treasure to the harvester, like old men offering to Death the virtue of their years.

Then the fields are full of children's laughter among the harvesters. And after that the hush, the solitude, and slow and bowed like mourners the gleaners trailing across the misty autumn stubble.

This was nearly done with at Silver Ley. For to grow corn at ten shillings a sack was speedy ruination. In the old days wages were considered to be on a generous scale if they equalled the price of a sack of wheat. Each labourer "took a coomb of wheat home on his back every Friday evening." But now, as Mr. Chilgrove, a farmer of five hundred acres near by, cried to me in dismay, standing hot-faced in his stack-yard after thrashing, among the mounds of straw that lately had been thatched ricks, "now he takes three sacks home on his back—and I've got twelve men: in the old days if you thrashed a couple of hundred coombs you expected it to fill a tidy gap—but now, why it don't go nowhere, and you've hardly seen the back of the thrashing tackle afore you've got to fetch it into your yard again and out with a whole lot more."

But in this respect I was really better off than my neighbours. There had been a possibility of my acquiring an extra field to my farm, and I had mentioned it to Bob Chilgrove. "My boy!" He jumped out with it in his sudden way, laying his hand flat upon the air for emphasis, "Don't you do nothin' of the sort. You're better off by half as you are. The less land you've got the better nowadays."

To cut costs on an arable farm of five hundred acres without letting it go to ruin was very difficult, or to

42

increase production without adding to them. But fifty acres was a much more flexible unit, and after the previous harvest I had sat down to ponder what should be done to cope with the times. I had done fairly well recently by getting calves to suckle my cows instead of milking, separating and making butter. They grew quickly like this, and were soon ready for the butcher with little expense to me. I put more land down to grass, bought another cow, and after weaning the calves in relays would let them run on the meadows, feeding to them also, meanwhile, beans and barley-meal and chaff which I grew on the little arable land remaining. I sold them in "bunches" (as they say) of half a dozen at a time as growing cattle. And very pretty they looked, for I took care that the calves I bought matched one another. However bad times may be, a choice lot will always command a fair price, for with those round a sale ring, as with the shopman's lady customer, a tempting appearance has an illogical influence. For instance, there is always a preference for roan cattle, and six of these all of level height, "with their tails well set up," make for brisk bidding. "Pretty little bunch," I heard two otherwise hard-headed farmers or dealers murmur as they paused by the pen; or, "Choice little lot, that," and then much whispering into the palms of their hands. No, they are not just business machines, the farmers that throng the market; there is pride of ownership. Each has a kind of old baronial pride in his home and fields, to put a face of prosperity on his independence—and he will pay for his pride, his soul's narcotic, almost as long as he can afford to pay for his tobacco. And what looks better from the road, and what can more cheer his heart as he goes to and fro, even in adverse times, than a herd of cattle all of the same size and colour among the trees in his meadow?

Then, again, there was poultry; and here the farmer's pride had suffered a blow indeed. For poultry he had always considered beneath his notice; poultry was a woman's occupation; it was completely ignored in his account-keeping. If his wife cared to rear chickens for pocket-money for herself, she was welcome to— he gave her the largesse of his barn from which to feed them. Bob Chilgrove frankly endured them for his wife's sake: I have heard him swear when they have jumped in over the lower barn door during breakfast and scrapped a heap of seed-wheat all about the floor. Or, coming to his reaper-and-binder after it had stood for eleven months in the cart-shed, he would find it smothered with their droppings and maybe a broody hen ensconced in the seat. As the eggs were collected only when a yard-boy had some odd moments, and nests might be anywhere, it is small wonder that eggs imported from the farther hemisphere were often to be preferred to those from the farms of Benfield St. George.

But, as the price of corn continued to fall, the regular arrival of the egg-collecting van, and the pound notes on the kitchen table, became more significant. At first Bob scratched his head and said, "Yes, I reckon I could make poultry pay if they didn't cost me anything for food." The happily married must always, I notice, have their bone of good-humoured contention, for it just wrings the cord of joy to be at beloved enmity— and these depredations on the barn-store were theirs.

His wife was fair-haired, blue-eyed, small and energetic, always teasing him, always laughing to get his broad red face puckered into slow bewilderment. But in this it became more than a joke, and she stroked his thin flat hair as he lumped himself into a chair one day on returning from market and gazed at the fire like one who had been dealt a blow—as he had indeed, having been refused a bid for his sample of corn on the one hand, and on the other hearing talk of how So-and-So, a substantial farmer, was going in for poultry on a large scale, and Such-and-Such, who had done so a year or two ago, had a weekly turnover now of some large and whispered figure.

Such topsy-turvy times as set this womanish occupation above the commanding work of cultivation of his wide acres "had him fair beat altogether."

Then there was a neighbour's wife whom he disliked and had largely blamed for his wife's, to him, mistaken zest for poultry rearing. "When they two get together —well, you know how women's tongues wag at any time—why, they jabber, jabber about them old hens worse than a couple of higglers. I have to go out of the house—that's the truth." All the words of scorn he had uttered and now had to take back!

One day he said to me, "I hate the old hens—but I shall have to take to 'em, I reckon."

Soon after, I found a smart young man in a drill overall walking about where not long since had been old labourers with bent bodies but nimble hands, while two laying-houses of great length were going up in two ten-acre fields. Mrs. Chilgrove woke up one morning to find that the business had been taken out of her hands completely. The dismissed labourers who had ploughed and harvested these fields for many years took to sticks and old-age pensions, and walked about together, pausing awhile to watch the great new venture going forward, murmuring "That's a rum 'un; that do be a rum 'un to me, and no mistake," and continuing slowly on toward their graves.

This is a case typical of many farmers; so that more and more the fields ·came to resemble factory sites, with these long, low poultry-sheds in the middle of them. And in the market at Stambury the talk came to be of such technical matters as incubators, battery brooders, sex-links, and the Mendelian theory, where before it had been of the corn being "winter-proud," or "wonderful unreg'lar," or "fair perished with the frost."

I had already abandoned the old haphazard barn-door poultry-keeping at Silver Ley—it had been my first move towards reorganisation—but as my paddocks were small I used houses to accommodate fifty hens each, as these were more easily moved, and therefore, I think, healthier.

Mrs. Chilgrove, deprived of her hobby (being a woman, the personal touch was everything to her, and she lost interest in hens treated as egg-factories), immediately took to bees—creatures which her husband hated even more than hens—and feared!

There were spheres of influence—mine the farm, Nora's the house—but in the garden they and we met. Farmers, they say, are not gardeners, but my love is in the tilling of the soil, and now the garden became almost the only place where one could meddle with the earth. What little the plough was used it was given into Walter's hands, as I didn't attempt to make him expert at over middle-age in the intricacies of scientific egg-production. Soon, however, that substantial friendship of wood and steel matured between me and my spade—but he was a friend in smaller compass, and a friend of half-hours and snatched interludes. He became to me, the thought of him waiting for me sentry-still in the half-dug plot by the orchard, even as the thought of a good book waiting open at the page by the fireside. For I confess that this intensive poultry-keeping seemed to me a soul-less affair, however necessary; monotonous, weather-immune, after the task of blending the forces of the air and the earth that is the arable farmer's. *That* was all woven around with Nature sporting herself in a thousand different ways, and taking her freedom with everything I did. With a new leaf the trimmed hedge would laughingly deny my ultimate power; my rising wheat was just the thing, Nature said, to house her

voles, and, though I ploughed up her weeds, she would
send her birds after me in a flock with a sweeping gesture,
pretending that I was turning the earth expressly at
her bidding, on behalf of her hungry ones.

But at these hens serving life-sentences in the egg-
factory one felt her smile of forbearance turn to a frown
of displeasure—and as I guessed, and as she always
does when outraged, she sent a retribution in the form
of disease. For a mysterious form of paralysis has
lately been reported, which afflicts these "forced"
pullets just when they should be about to lay, and the
verdict seems to be that their constitutions can't stand
being made into egg-machines.

Nature may be "red in tooth and claw"; there is a
ruthlessness in human inventiveness which seems to
shock her, nevertheless.

Still, there was the garden-sanctum; and there her
robin awaited me in the old spirit upon the handle of
my spade, or glowing up from the brown earth, commanding me—his bright eye was—to turn another
clod.

It was a joy to be there within the close quickset
hedge, perhaps the rarer because of this mechanisation
of life besieging us to the very doors, working together—
no, not together, but at different jobs, yet within such
easy distance as made a conversation of silence. The
human heart, much-travelling in the dust of disappointment, must somewhere have its secret spring of hope.
In scenes of man there was no cheer just now—but,
unconfessed, we drew refreshment from our shared
plot. It was, I think, our "start in life."

Not that our separate spheres were altogether un-
shared. And in this we differed from the indigenous
convention of our farming neighbours—a separatist
convention which, surely, was the last vestige of Vic-
torianism. Thus Bob Chilgrove spoke of having

helped Polly put down "her" stair-carpet. Polly told us one day that another of "his" horses had gone lame. And so on.

Nora outraged convention by coming out into the field and helping me plant potatoes—laying them in the furrows while Walter ploughed the earth over them. This was another of my side-lines. I had several acres in a declivity which were called "new land," having been reclaimed from swamp some time within a century ago. The earth was black and very close and friable. "It plough wonderful 'numb,'" Walter exclaimed, coming to it after the clean-cut, clayey furrows of the rest of the farm. Corn was apt to grow too much straw there, but roots and potatoes would "grow like elder." So we tried market-gardening it, with a fair amount of success. One year I sold potatoes at ten pounds a ton. Next year there was a glut, and they were only worth about two pounds ten shillings; so I boiled them up for the pigs. They were a gamble, but in a small way and over a period of years were well worth it.

It was sheltered down on the "new land"; the April sun shone full on us there. Nora and I each went with a pail of "sets" and laid them along in the furrow, and later Walter came and hitched the horses to the plough and covered them in.

For the plough is not quite left out of the spring seeding. Its first job after harvest is to ridge up those acres destined for next year's root crop; and in the spring it returns to them when their toughness is reduced by winter frosts to a rich sift, as of molehills.

The ridges were split over the potatoes. The plough floundered through the shifty soil as through soot; it drove up, almost smothering the breast, which could hardly push it aside. The plough was like a boat whose prow foundered in the spray; there was nothing for the coulter to cut nor the share to cut—no terra firma; it could only go nosing through the soft mass of earth like a mole, with Walter all the while leaning over it in an attitude of emergency, and keeping up a crooning chant of admonition, loudening to a clear command as one horse or the other inclined to error. That is what he meant by saying it ploughed "numb"—this dark smother of fertility that covered our seed potatoes in the luring April weather.

Nora was quick—her fingers worked dexterously—and I had some trouble to keep up with her, though I did not admit it. I believe she was racing me all that first day on the quiet, for we were both dead tired that night, and we wondered to each other why we were so sleepy, and voted it must be the air or smell of the soil or spring or something; but said nothing about having been working at higher pressure than usual. The next day I could stand the pace no longer, but covered my failure by straightening myself and walking over the field to have several minutes' discussion with Walter. This put me well behind, and by the time I stooped to it again Nora was at the other end of the field, so there was no question of keeping level. It is curious how two people working together—I have noticed it at hoeing—act as a spur each to the other. Do what you will, a silent spirit of competition asserts itself, and you find you are going, or attempting to go, ever a little faster. The one at your side has the effect of a pacer—drawing you on as by a hypnotic spell which lulls the more violent sense of effort.

But Walter had noticed. "A woman's always quicker than a man at such jobs as 'tater setting. They can bend easier, and they're nimbler-handed nor we. My missis can pick peas twice as quick as I can. But there," he added, in male extenuation, "a woman's always handling 'taters, so she ought to know the way on't."

But Walter's first surprise at seeing Nora stooping

49

in the potato field with me—flushed and hatless (who in the country ever goes out without a hat?)—I shall not forget. I am sure his opinion of it all was—as retailed to the village—"She rule he, that's a fact." And village rumour can be more fantastic than a dream. Mrs. Chilgrove told us she had been informed we went to bed at seven o'clock each night; the basis of this was that Nora kept a light burning upstairs after dark as a matter of convenience, and the passer-by had jumped to the conclusion that we were getting ready for bed!

Some people are annoyed at being gossiped about in the village, but it rather amused us, and Nora did not mind fomenting it in little ways. Thus, when a friend with a baby came to stay with us in the summer, the day after her arrival Nora wheeled the child down through the village while the mother rested. That night we expected to see a red light in the sky over Benfield! And when Mrs. Chilgrove, the following afternoon, cried, "Do you know what I heard this morning?" we said no, but we could guess.

A lady and gentleman took a large house near by, and sent round to me one day (I being the nearest poultry farmer) for a chicken. When it was killed and plucked, I sent Walter over with it. He was met at the door by a "rum-looking fellow," he told me. "He jabbered that quick I couldn't understand one word he said."

"What was he—the butler?" I suggested.

"Aye, summat like that—but he were a foreigner."

"What country does he belong to, do you reckon?"

Walter thought awhile, then shook his head slowly. "I reckon he's Chinese."

Later I saw the butler, who was a Frenchman, speaking broken English.

So Nora wore the breeches, invading that outdoor sphere where even the most henpecked farmer's word is law!

But then Walter did not see my invasion of her sphere on occasion. He did not know that it was "our" furniture as well as "our" potatoes!

Each bit of it, almost, represents some lean-shadowed day's end at Stambury, our big, old, twelve-miles-away market town. And how this double outlook on life had altered the view of that place, too. A place whose important cattle market and its attendant inns, offices, agricultural merchants, had a whole street to themselves; whose Corn Exchange advanced its pediment right into the central square, graven with Ceres offering her sheaves and the ploughman resting beside his plough. For corn was the vital gold of Stambury, and every coin passed across its counters had at one time been owned as cattle or grain.

When I had been a bachelor farmer, market-day had meant chiefly the bustle of the cattle market till dinner, and afterwards the humming hive of the Corn Exchange. All hurly-burly—then home. But now, towards the end of the day, how the roughnesses were smoothed off and the clamour quietened, till there was only the tapping of our heels on the paving of some sequestered Georgian square as we went peering into old shops, charmed out of reality by the opiate evening sky. Just as though the town had reserved those frail balconies and angles of mossed wall for some such contingency as this light hand laid upon the young go-ahead's check sleeve.

So the soul of the town was not, as I had thought, its breeches pocket, but those retired parts where birds sang in the tall gardens, those grey façades, plain and proud, behind which it sat remembering.

Contrary to the immemorial practice governing relations of farmer and wife—that they parted on arrival and only met again at the car for departure—business done, we would go sauntering off together into those quarters.

This whatever it was between us that put a strangeness upon common things, surprised us also into explorations beyond the town into country I knew nothing of despite my ten years' acquaintance with the district, for the farmer does not go far afield unless it be to market or to see a horse or a cow—certainly not to see a reed shaken with the wind, all on an impulse caught from the twinkling young willow-leaves.

Our diary of that April tells of many such days, half-days, evenings, when we went out just for the pleasure of having no need to arrive anywhere—the gesture of freedom that all life made in common with us after winter, when everything gives a leap a little beyond itself in delight or rarity or power: the lark ascends to the clouds—the bedridden old man gets up and sits in his porch—the cankered cherry-bough breaks into flowers of sheerest texture.

Here I loiter, bedtime long past, dipping into those pages, with the illusion of Time being my slave by the way the months dance back and forth as I turn the leaves.

Thanks be to old Bloomfield, the peasant poet of a hundred years ago, for this day that shines with a wan reflection of itself, like a pressed flower, from the page —the day we went seeking his shade about Honington and Sapiston and Euston—his birthplace, and in appearance even to this day the territory of patronage.

We had been reading his *Farmer's Boy*, bought for sixpence out of a dark, chaotic little shop in Stambury —a book which sold by its thousands a hundred years ago—and then we turned to seek a meal—for it struck one—and found a low-windowed shop next to the bookshop where a great ham blushed at us, and a varnished joint of beef sat on white American cloth behind a bodyguard of four beer-bottles, interspersed with tomatoes. The price of dinner, writ large, was one and sixpence, or, alternatively, two shillings. The substantial honesty of the window display tempted us, as though Bloomfield's account of harvest labours had given us appropriate appetite, and in we went—through the shop and around the counter into an inner room. It was a low room with a ceiling askew and random windows—a room in which the art of the grainer had been allowed such play it was as though one of the profession had paid for his meal in service. The wainscoting, the beams, the doors, all shone brown as a horse-chestnut newly broken from its shell, and upon them the swirls, flecks, and complicated eddies that may have been the grain, perhaps, of that Tree of Knowledge of Good and Evil which grew in Eden, but of none known on earth since then.

Here a serving-woman came to us and asked, did we require a hot or a cold dinner? We answered, cold—we should like some of that ham and that beef we had seen, and a bottle of the beer and some of the tomatoes.

Her next question was, did we require a large or a small dinner?

Content that the custom of the house should take its course, we did not prevaricate for explanation, but ordered, I a large dinner, Nora a small.

While we waited, a man came in with two women, and all ordered large, hot dinners. And a little after there wavered on the threshold a very old, solitary man. At first we thought he was in doubt about entering, but it was not that but the infirmity of his gait that delayed him. With two sticks he steered quadrupedally between the tables and sank down with a sigh upon a bench against the wall. With screwed, sunk eyes, as though the light and traffic of day were too much for him now, he laid his sticks together, undid first one coat, then another—though this was one of the fairest days of spring—arriving at last past a woollen cardigan at a stout waistcoat with flapped pockets, into one of which his fingers fumbled and brought forth a purse as shrivelled as his own skin,

53

and out of the purse a florin, which he held before him with his trembling hand for a minute; then, as the serving-woman was busy elsewhere, laid it before him on the table as witness, presumably, that despite his poor appearance he was able to pay for his dinner.

Now the woman came in with a large plate quite covered with meat, which she put before Nora. I indicated that it was I who had ordered the large dinner, but the woman said "That's the small dinner," and departed for mine, leaving us in awed speculation. The plate I received was quite as big as a dish, but though the china was thick and plain the meat upon it was a miracle of fine carving, a delicate fabric, slice overlapping slice, the last overhanging the edge of the plate, beef mingled with ham whose lean was as though trimmed with white lace. So when we had sliced the tomatoes, crackled the crust of bread, and poured out the beer, we had as handsome a meal before us as any could have wished. Hungry as we were, Nora confessed to a momentary pang that such a harmony must be destroyed to be fulfilled.

"I wish," I said, "that I could carve meat as sheer as this; it must be a real joy to have the art so perfect."

"I wish you could," sighed Nora, for my attempts on the joint were vigorous but unlovely, and I knew that it would always slither about like that, and I should cut first a thick slice and then many little choppy ones trying to cut a thinner, and that the joint would always get out of shape through my repeatedly going for the easy places, and that I should never, never, never make a carver. Nora, though, carved very nicely. As soon as the knife was in her hands it became six times as sharp, the joint stood its ground like a man, and those obscure obstructions, sudden bones and artfully concealed skewers, were not encountered. But if there is one thing fatal to the proper harmony of a household it is for the woman to carve, for, if you have noticed, in whatever house the woman carves it is she who rules —she who looks up trains, chooses the children's names —and schools—and answers the telephone. From this first delegation of his duty to his wife the man gradually loses all initiative in the family's affairs, loses touch with it to such an extent that it becomes matriarchal, and he retires to find himself ultimately a stranger and a lodger in his own house.

So I persevered, hacking my way to domestic domination, as Nora agreed I must; for what is even a lifetime of spoilt joints to the inversion of the marriage relation?

We all had our dinners now; the old man, the man, and his two wives, cousins, or aunts. Theirs were hot heaped stew with potatoes at the apex. We all ate, it appeared, with equal appetite in the low little wooden room.

After that we made our way, with Bloomfield in my pocket, to Honington where he was born, losing all other than local traffic, and in our leisure allowing the farmer's boy—caught hedgerow-dreaming—all the time he needed to move his load of hay to the side of the narrow road to let us go past. The sense of getting lost to all reminders of the width of the world, and the closing in about us of the purely local, was deepened by the many twists and right-angled bends of the road, so that when we came to "Cairo Café" written on a little shop, the association was quite as odd as the Saracen's Head of Sir Roger de Coverley. One imagined just how the villager had gone to the wars, and returning to the same green lane with its foam of sheep's parsley, had blazoned the fading strangeness of his experience over his lintel for souvenir, or to refresh his belief in it.

It was hay-time, and that was quite all the traffic we met—yes, let it be recorded that a hundred years after he lived there, from the time we left the main road to the time we arrived at Bloomfield's native village we met only horse-drawn loads of hay sighing past us as they brushed the hedges.

We sat by the 'weir of Sapiston, among the fields he worked in and wrote about, where the rushing of the water could not quite drown the voice of a blackbird singing and swaying recklessly on the windy willow-top. On one side the chattering shallows dappled with brisk light, where children paddled and caught up the water with their hands, and sparrows sat flirting it over their wings. On the other side the stream ran deep and dark to its abrupt fall, and there pike hung revealed, or moved through the light from shadow into shadow. Occasionally a labourer who might have been Bloomfield himself parted the branches on the opposite bank to dip his pail. Occasionally a load to the mill splashed through the ford where the children dabbled. Cattle nosed in the little runnel that twined among willows through the meadow, a clear current with a floor of sand and alabaster pebbles fluttering thin pennons of water-weed.

We returned up the mill lane, the barefoot children following, brown dust as sandals to their wet feet. We viewed the church and found it all but identical with the hundred-year-old engraving in our book— by chance a whiff of gale came suddenly with a heavy cloud, bending boughs and silvering the coltsfoot, overcasting the day with the gloom of the picture. Light broke out again from the cloud's flaming border, for a minute on only the church. Its sumptuous porch shone with a cathedral quality which looked strange among these peasant cottages, where all depended on the soil and their labour for a living, where every curve, however luxuriant—scythe or plough or wagon-rail— was primarily one of use.

For, even as in Bloomfield's time, here

THE CHERRY TREE

Unassisted through each toilsome day,
With smiling brow the plowman cleaves his way,
Draws his fresh parallels and, widening still,
Treads slow the heavy dale or climbs the hill.

I reflected that only a ploughboy-poet would have
applied the word "heavy" to the dale, with memories
of the wet earth loading his boots in winter.

But we travelled on to Euston, a neighbouring but
quite different village, starting our car, whose motion
infected the children to run alongside. Our progress
was slow, for in the village street we found ourselves
fronting a charge of unharnessed plough-horses that
were being driven from their stables to a meadow down
the road. The walls echoed with their hooves; they
were spirited with release from toil and the lifting of
the yokes from their necks; they jostled, flattened back
their ears, and snapped at one another's manes. The
wind followed them; they moved in the midst of the
sunlit dust that rose from their hooves, they themselves
glowing autumnal in the declining rays which misted
them to the likeness of an allegory. They were like
a river in spate rushing towards us down the street,
parting and racing by on either side. The children
were not frightened of them, but stood and let them
jostle by. Last came a ploughman riding bareback
on an old horse, his lean body straight and his legs
dangling. Even the old horse, finding himself left behind,
lumbered into a trot. The meadow gate stood open;
the horses crowded through, overrunning at the turn
and striking sparks from the hard road. Feeling the
turf under them, they threw up their heels and thundered
away into freedom. The old horse, the rider having
dismounted, looked after them, standing just within
the gate. For him it was enough to be just within the
gate. He shook his mane and bent his head to the
grass.

So we passed out of Sapiston; our speed increasing,
the children were left behind. They stood at the end
of the path with feathery grasses in their hands that
they had plucked as they went. Then they turned
their backs on us and began a new game.

For a little we were beside fields where men hoed
and gathered clover-hay, or ploughed the sudden
wintry square of a bare fallow. But then the country
of labour gave place to park and woodland; the river
that turned the mill at Sapiston became a trim reach
of ornamental water, a white stone bridge spanning
it with a lissom bow giving a cool light of stone under
the tree shadows, a Græco-Georgian temple crowning
a knoll, generous wood-rides, generous turf by the
roadside, all fenceless, open, undulating. Over the
river was a rose-garden right to its verge, and beyond
stood Euston Hall, the seat of the Duke of Grafton,
who had been Bloomfield's benefactor,

Lord of pure alms and gifts that wide extend,
The farmer's patron and the poor man's friend,

but for whom his poems would never have gained
publication. These two places, the peasant Sapiston
and the noble Euston, were a natural monument to
that old system of patronage which enabled the farm
lad of delicate constitution to win fame with a poem
which sold twenty thousand copies in two years, of
which Bloomfield's sister wrote from America, "It is
making a great bustle here," and which was even
translated into German.

Deep in the trees stood Euston village—a few toy-
neat cottages, each with its open greensward before
it—overshadowed by the dark wing-spread of the
ancient cedars. A flock of sheep came glimmering
through the trees towards us, behind them two bearded
shepherds in light brown corduroys. We stopped the

car to let them by, and became an island in a fleecy flood. They swamped round us, confused and frightened. So dense was the flock that they crowded right to the verge of the river, and there was a danger lest some should be forced in. The shepherds, their crooks in their hands, were wrestling thigh-deep in the torrent of fear which pushed and pushed against them towards the river. The black faces and smoky eyes of the sheep were desperately upturned from the foam of fleeces, as though drowning in it. While the shepherds worked they kept calling to their dogs, and each shepherd's dog attended to his own master alone—crouching alert or running and barking according to his commands. For a minute all was shouting, scuffling, and bleating under the shade of the giant cedars—then the sheep were past safely, and vanished, the whole multitude, leaving the place quiet to the twittering of a sparrow.

We had tea at Burnham Water, a brook by which Bloomfield admits to loitering as a boy when sent on errands by his master. And there we left his young ghost, dabbling his feet in the stream, and, incidentally, wasting his master's time.

That day which we spent in travelling many miles, the first petal of the iris by the porch of Silver Ley had spent in creeping out of the thick-swathed bud; it hung out like a flag to greet us on our return.

CHAPTER VI

THERE are some that are called in the country "little men," men who own each some one thing—an engine, horse and van, gravel pit—and contrive, or rather endeavour in these hard times, to earn a living with it. One, a woodman who made rough parts for the agriculturist such as whipple-trees and plough-handles, came to me on a Saturday morning and asked if I could let him have ten shillings "on account" of some things I had ordered from him. He began with that quiet and apologetic voice which portends the asking of a favour. He explained, "I want to pay my butcher's bill so I can get a bit more meat, and then I'd like to buy an ounce of baccy, and then," he said brightly as I drew forth the note, "I shall be set up for the week-end."

He thanked me, and went off pleased at his temporary respite from insolvency. I marvelled at the modest consolations of hard times, that ten shillings had the power to "set up" a man with a cheerful week-end, and buffer him with mere hours, as with melting snow, against waiting cares.

That creaking which sounded all day from the spinney was not one bough groaning against another in the wind, but the croaking of a carrion crow on her nest, brooding the eggs. It was a harsh monotonous noise, and sounded sinister among the pervading grace and

lightness of spring. As indeed it was, for with the
hatching of the young increasing depredations were
to be expected on my chicks. I had already lost quite
a number. The crow haunted our buildings like a vile
omen; one would ever come round a corner to find her
shadowing silently away with some small prey, or
slinking, for all one's yell, only a little way off to wait
her further opportunity.

I must kill her or she would cause me infinite loss,
and I kept my gun constantly by me. But the carrion
crow is craftier than the rook; it is as though she
expects you to be lying in wait for her, and knows
the power of a gun to kill at a distance. As I walked
to the spinney one day I saw a single drop of blood upon
a pebble. It was new, wet. It shone up at me like a
single eye among the universal green of spring—lonely,
mysterious, lethal. For days I sat hours at a time in
the spinney. The tree was tall and straight, and the
crow's nest was right at the top of it, a thick tangle
of sticks.

It became a duel of watchfulness and elusion. A
single shot, well aimed, would rid me of her and her
brood, but to get that second's opportunity took hours
of stone-stillness, waiting. She had to leave her nest
and she had to return; she must feed, but she must not
let her eggs get cold; my only chance was to get her at
the moment she left or returned to the nest.

I wore a green cap and a green coat, the less easily
to be seen; but she saw me. She watched me, I knew,
from her eyrie, as I watched it. To sit thus still in a
wood may sound monotonous; but no—those were
fascinating hours; the wood came to life. If you can
sit and let your body grow into a wood for stillness,
become part of the tree-trunk you lean against, then
only you see the wood as it really is, that it is not trees
—they are only the roof and pillars—but a people.
Rabbits sported about me; pheasants strolled like fine

gentlemen in a park; and once a woodcock came walking down the ride-way, waddling awkwardly with his great beak thrust out before him. A fox padded along it, and squatted a few yards from me sniffing the air, vaguely uneasy of a sudden, looking at me but still not seeing I was a man. A white owl swooped so close to me I felt the beat of its wing in the air, and was surprised by the momentary illusion of a giant furry moth. I think he was the minion of that black witchbird, for in that second when my eyes were withdrawn from her nest she flew from the thick boughs whence she had been watching and waiting, right across the clearing and into it. So I knew my chance was over for that day.

It is not difficult to believe in the supernatural, sitting long alone in a wood; the wandering airs grow half-articulate, and one is aware of the upsurging life in the trunks of the trees. I learnt there what may have been the origin of the belief in fairies; for in the dusk the bobbing white tails of the rabbits are like the wantoning of little delicate wings.

One might believe in the prescience of that unholy bird, too, with her croak echoing dolefully through the place; for the one time she swept out before me within easy range my gun happened to be at half-cock! Otherwise she would choose the very moment when my eyes were lured from their vigil to make her dash; she'd come and go like a shadow after my hours of waiting.

I had her at last, though. I had given her up, one evening, thinking she must have alighted in the nest unperceived by me, when, stepping out of the wood, I found her flying straight towards me. She gave a cry and veered sharply, but she was right overhead, and she knew that her time was come. I raised my gun and shot her full in the head; she crashed into the wood like a stone and never moved. She lay on her back,

caught up in a bramble-thicket, her wicked claws curled
empty in the air, while a dead chick dropped from them
from branch to branch on to the ground.

Next the pigeons began their depredations, picking
the hearts out of our clover plants and stuffing their
crops full of our seed-corn. So the farmers of Benfield,
as was the yearly custom, came together and organised
shooting-parties. It was impossible seriously to deplete
the flocks that infested the country; the main intention
was to scare them away; the principle being, "We
don't mind what parish you settle in so long as it isn't
Benfield—go to Selbridge if you like"—while the farmers
of Selbridge, also organised with guns, said, "Back
you go—back to Benfield."

We stationed ourselves in all the woods and spinneys
towards dusk, and whichever one the flock attempted
to roost in, drove them off. On our side of the valley
there were Bob Chilgrove, Joe Boxted (who had an
old single-barrel gun, but neither game- nor gun-licence,
and "be damned to 'em"), and the three sons of old
Will Russet, Major, Henry, and Reuben. Major was
middle-aged, tall and sombre—over-careful, over-steady;
Henry was given to clowning; but Reuben I liked best
because he was simply his own quiet self, substantial
and satisfying as a companion. The others were never
quite with you; the one took refuge in reserve, the other
in a burst of laughter. The one liked the mystery
of "business," had his paper open always at the financial
page, and though he had only a three-hundred-acre
farm implied other irons in the fire; spoke cryptically
of anyone mentioned, as though he knew a great deal
more than he'd say about him, always loved to be
whispering in low tones to someone, and made the Corn
Exchange a court of imaginary subterfuges.

The other, who had two hundred acres, was equally
elusive, with his fitful laugh, and both attached undue

importance to anything they alone knew, as though exclusiveness made it paramount.

Reuben had only about a hundred acres, being the youngest, and hardly a fair start at that, for farming was turning to go downhill when he started just after the war. The others had not much of an opinion of him as a business man, their idea of business being maximum negotiation over anything bought or sold. Reuben would be working in his fields while they glided by in their cars importantly to market; but he didn't mind. He confessed he disliked markets and preferred to be doing a job on the land, and I agreed with him.

There were many belts and woods in the vale of Benfield, and if any were left untenanted it would frustrate the efforts of the whole party, as the pigeons would alight there undisturbed; so considerable organisation was necessary even for an evening's pigeon shooting.

Some would be hunting and have to abandon the chase even in the middle of an exciting run, so as not to let their friends down; often without time for tea or change one would spring from the saddle into the car, and hasten to his post, so that any stroller might have come upon the unique spectacle of a man dressed for fox-hunting sitting in wait with a gun on his shoulder.

Part of our "beat" belonged to the miniature estate of old Captain Barkle. Nobody seemed to know of any connection he had had with either of the Services, only his appearance was spruce and bristly, and I can only think that the East Anglian love of an apt, and if possible military, title was responsible for his. He had grown so used to his old mare that he still hunted while she continued to carry him, but he had given up the gun, and we used to man his woods for him on these occasions.

Reuben called for me in his little rust-edged car, and we loitered along towards the woods, for it was one of those cloudless skies that hold the light like a drop of wine in a silver spoon. The sun still shone, and, it seemed, would continue to shine for hours. A bland glow bloomed last year's stubbles. It was like the aftermath of harvest, for ruinous grain prices had led many to set clover and grasses in their corn last year, which had not yet smothered the stubble.

"Look," cried Reuben, "look at the old devils, millions of 'em feeding on that clover." His sharp eyes had recognised that which to me looked like a grey shadow to be innumerable pigeons, and now mine also disintegrated it into motes, each a bird stuffing its crop with the tender centres of the young clover.

These should rise at last when the sun set and seek the shelter of the woods, and then no shelter should they find. But the sun could never set it seemed, nor this light change, turning all the landscape to haze, to shadow which over there was but mist, and there was a leafless wood.

Hares too there were, crouching in this gentle lap of earth, this plough-forsaken hollow, and pheasants and partridges, all consorting together for their evening feed, quite oblivious of us going by on the raised road. The car was used to rough ground, and jogged through a field gateway and round under lee of a stack, where we got out. We took our guns into the wood. There we parted after hanging our cartridge-satchels on some boughs under which a trap had been set for a stoat —a neat twig-palisaded path leading to tempting (to the stoat) remains of a rabbit which concealed the jaws of steel. Here we arranged to meet again and went off in opposite directions down the nave of the wood, the broad "glide-way." On either side the middle air was criss-crossed with bows of bramble and elder that threw up all their strength in a wild effort after the light, stretching lanky tendons that could not support the desperate aspiration to out-top the trees, and fell again, the tips back to the roots, with weakness. They sought in some places support from each other, bramble grappling bramble and both falling flat upon the earth.

But the first leaf-buds were already burst, and the air was alive as with flitting wings, was silently a-buzz with new life. The first pigeons came, but very high, wheeling in grey vortices and away elsewhere at sight of me, for the sun was still on the horizon.

I heard Joe Boxted shoot, for his gun made a curiously flat, dull thump as it went off, more like a blow than an explosion. Reuben's made the wood echo and next moment three pigeons came over me, one of which I brought down. If one stopped for pity? If one stopped to think about the creatures that preyed on our fields, the cool-voiced lustrous wood-pigeons? Once, in a hard winter, one sat upon a bough before me, being too starved with frost for fear, and I would not shoot; but this was spring, and the crops of the birds bulged out before them as they flew, they were so full, making their graceful shapes grotesque.

It was a quick shot and broke the wing; he tried to balance on a bough as he fell. For a moment he clung, but he had only one wing and could not achieve his balance. He crashed through the branches, one of his own down feathers in his beak. I gave him a merciful blow which caused the lid to flutter over the glowing eye, and the head to fall that had been held erect from the maimed body smothering in last year's leaves, had manfully watched my approach with that keen apprehensive spark; but now the head drooped forward on to the earth, and with the shuttering of the eye all the light seemed to go out of him, even the shimmer of his breast and neck, and the smooth-packed feathers to slacken, so that he became just a dead dull thing, and lost the quick gleam of his life.

But there were thousands of such creatures, all softly shaded colour into colour, even to the last feather, wheeling and seeking an arbour for their rest, which we were denying them because our corn and our clover it was that went to turn the glance of daylight into a rainbow upon breast and back, instead of to provide the things of daily use for us.

The stubble plain might have been sand, might have been a sweep of undulating desert from the covert wherein was already cold twilight, for the sun was even yet lambent on the fields. I heard others shooting, and each gun was characteristic. From the north there came always a double shot; that was Major; he was a poor hand with a gun and might be relied upon to need both barrels. From the east came the sharp, short crack of Bob Chilgrove's twenty-bore; he never used anything else about his farm, and always shot in the head. His father, he told me, had given him only a single-barrel gun to start with when a lad, because, he said, "That'll learn you to aim well first time and make spare of cartridges, as you'll not have a chance of a second shot." From the west came the thump of Joe Boxted's ancient piece of ordnance, and from the south Henry Russet's heavy twelve-bore, which had a punch like a boxer's and crashed and echoed all over the valley.

Next moment the pigeons would be overhead; the whole afterglow was stippled with their thousands. Lower they came, seeking this place last. One settled on a bough at the edge of the wood; others were attracted to him. They liked the fir trees, flopping heavily into the black foliage as into a nest, the branches lolling low with their weight. Here at last they thought they found rest; then Reuben's gun made the wood resound; the fir-tops seemed to spring into the air as the scared birds rose in a cloud. I brought down two as they started once more on their desperate pilgrimage. "But the dove found no rest for the sole of her foot." Again the several shots rang out from wood and wood, and the flock returned again to our wood, lower this time, and settling everywhere about us in the trees. My gun grew hot with shooting them before they would depart yet once more, rising in groups heavily and wearily now.

It was getting dark; a cock pheasant kept stuttering upon a bough where he had sat all through the bombardment, as though knowing that the calendar made him safe. I went to the edge of the wood and saw the fire flash from Henry Russet's gun.

The half-light that had driven the pigeons to our guns deepened now, and became their shelter, for they returned only a few at a time; many had already settled in other woods. Those that came here did so with impunity, as it was no longer possible to see them at all in the wood. They roosted quietly on the boughs just over my head.

The whole valley was silent now; I heard Reuben whistle, and went to the meeting-place where we had hung our satchels. We loaded ourselves with the dead birds and carried them to the car.

On our way home we met a bull with a five-barred gate on its horns standing in the middle of the road. It glowered at us through the bars and shook his head, and Reuben wisely brought the rusty little car to a halt.

"That's a handy thing to meet on a dark night," he said. I agreed. "That's Captain Barkle's bull," he said. "It's been standing so long in his yard it's got the master of everybody on the place."

Just then we heard female cries, and discovered half a dozen women who had been on their way home from market cowering in the ditch.

It appeared that the bull had been in the habit of breaking out and making free of the countryside, so that no one had dared walk on the road to the town after dark. It had smashed down the wooden shed in which it had been confined when young. But then it had been put into a brick-walled yard, and Captain Barkle had assured the village that the road was quite safe for them again. That had been but yesterday; and to-day the bull had walked out like Samson, carrying the gate on its head.

Captain Barkle had all along pooh-poohed the idea that the bull was dangerous. It only needed handling, he said; a little intelligent handling. The men, he said, started by being frightened of the thing, treated it as something dangerous, and naturally it got rattled. The secret was to treat it in a confident, friendly way, and show you weren't afraid of it. He implied that he, personally could do anything he liked with the bull.

We packed the women all into the little car—some of them were very wide—and approached the enemy in low gear, for "I'm not going to stop here all night for a dam' bull," Reuben said. "I want my tea, and the car's insured."

The car made such a noise at full throttle in low gear that even the bull was taken aback. Reuben switched the headlamps suddenly into his eyes and he drew back, whether to rush at us or get out of our way I don't know, for next moment we squeezed by. The women in the back all shrieked as the bull's head gazed in at the side and blew a vast snort on them, and the two in front shrieked in sympathy. I was glad we had only a mile to go to the village; what with angles of shopping-baskets in each rib and hundredweights of human flesh pushing me against an insecure door, it was worse than "Uncle Tom Cobley and all."

The rest of the story I heard from Reuben later. It appeared that the bull had not been recaptured till next morning; or rather, it was not so much recaptured as returned of its own accord. It trotted up the front drive in fact, and arrived at the front door simultaneously with the groom and the Captain's horse from the stables. The groom leaped into the saddle he had prepared for his master and cantered off, leaving the bull in possession. The bull pounded the gravel, worried his head at some scarlet geraniums, tore them up, and sat down on the ornamental bed. The shrubberies became full of scared white faces of people who ought to have been doing something about it but dared not.

Then the Captain slammed a window up and put out his head. "What's all this?" he cried. "What are you all gaping there for like lunatics?"

A minute later he opened the front door and walked out; he was dressed in pink, ready for hunting. He went boldly over to the bull, saying, "Now, old fellow, up you get." The bull was up and at him in no time, and had him pinned against the wall of the house. The gamekeeper had the presence of mind to run forward then and shoot the bull in the head.

The Captain, who was shaken but otherwise un-hurt, insisted on going hunting as he had intended; ordered them to drag the carcase into the barn, and set off forthwith. Nothing more was done about it for several days, when it was hoisted up and hung from a beam. The Captain, being Hunt Secretary, was very busy propitiating poultry farmers, then he got a chill, and when he recollected the dead bull again he ordered the butcher to be sent for to cut it up. An appeal from his pet charity—an orphanage—had arrived by that morning's post. The Captain intended to send a great present of meat to the orphans, and had hampers fetched.

The butcher said he never wanted another job like that as long as he lived, and as for packing it, he'd leave the Captain's men to do that. The men filled their pipes with the strongest shag to accomplish it. The groom said the old nag galloped all the way to the station with the loaded gig, trying to turn a following wind into a head one. The porters rushed the hampers to the farthest end of the platform, and the passengers congregated at the other end till the train arrived. One and all gave thanks that they were not orphans.

CHAPTER VII

THE evenings lengthened, and the time came when it was light enough to walk round the farms after tea, which Bob Chilgrove and I did regularly in the late spring. We walked over the two farms as though they had been one, and while on my land I would act as guide and he as commentator, as soon as we stepped over the boundary our positions would be reversed; his stick would begin to gesture and mine just to poke and prod.

We reckoned the whole distance round the land was five miles, but of course did not cover it all in a single walk; we tended mostly to keep to those parts of it where we still continued our arable activities. Compared to the daily variations of the naked soil, the grassland was like a petrification of our agriculture. We used often to marvel, as we walked about, what grassland farmers found to do all day. "Lazy man's farming," Bob called it.

Once he had come upon a farm right away among the moors, he told me. And he planted down his stick so emphatically it made a hole in the ground, and stopped and turned to me. I, following the custom to which I had grown used, stopped and turned to him. For our walks were by no means continuous; it was really a wonder we ever got as far as we did, because when anything surprising or emphatic occurred to him, Bob always stopped dead in the path to tell me of it. So there we stood while he told me of this benighted place he found when taking a holiday. "Nobody wouldn't ever find it unless they were lost," he said. The farmer was sitting in his porch with the last Sunday's newspaper. As soon as he found that Bob also was a farmer he invited him in, gave him whisky and milk, and, like most lonely people, talked a great deal.

When Bob asked him what sort of farming he did about there, he said sheep-farming. He had thousands of sheep, he said, though not so much as a bleat had Bob heard anywhere about the place. "I'll show you my sheep," he said, and went out into the porch where two dogs lay. He spoke to them, and they immediately leaped up and ran off. They watched the two dogs racing each other right into the distance till they disappeared from sight over the horizon of a great hill. Then they went back into the stone kitchen and had another glass of whisky and milk.

Presently a multitudinous sound, as of the wind, was heard, and the two dogs reappeared at the doorway with their tongues lolling. The farmer led Bob out, and now the whole house was surrounded with sheep right up to the threshold. "I never saw such a sight in my life," Bob concluded; and then we proceeded on our walk.

Sometimes Nora came with us. This had rather nonplussed Bob at first, as the convention was that the "ladies" stayed in the house and talked domestic matters, while the men walked about the fields and prodded the earth, discussing whether they or the cloud that had just swallowed the sun would have the next say in the matter.

But for her ability to look gracefully silken on occasion, Nora secretly would have received the name of "tomboy," which to Bob Chilgrove and the farming community generally meant something like a hermaphrodite.

And that is as is natural to the farmer. For it adds

a relish to his roughness to be met by smiling fragility at the porch; it adds something to the firmness of his grasp on reins and gun and plough, to have fingers sewing fine things by the fire; there is a pleasure in his gaitered legs and nailed boots being abashed before the pointed feet of his wife, who treads with high-heeled, artificial delicacy; the awkwardness of his in the drawing-room fills him with a secret awe of fineness; it is like a vista through a doorway through which he can't quite squeeze himself. Then how excellent, after the soft flattery of the carpet, the ring of his heel on the step again and the challenge of the outer air!

Even roughness nowadays is refined in that it likes to play with the lure of smoothness.

However, Bob Chilgrove admitted Nora into the mystery of agriculture; finding, to his surprise, that she could get over a ditch more nimbly than he could. At first, though, she would cry out in alarm as we set large, square feet on a field of barley-blades just peeping through the tilth.

"Shan't we hurt it?"

Bob would smile indulgently, not without a certain pleasure at this womanly—rather than "tomboy"—instinct to protect the young and frail. He'd shake his head, treading full on a row with each foot, like a boy doing it for mischief, and twist on his heel, replying, "No, that won't do it any harm."

He enjoyed, I think, taking us where all that day the harrows had been tearing through the wheat, heaping the earth over the young plants till the rows were hardly visible, to hear her compassionately exclaim. It came to be quite a regular thing, this bait of surprise he prepared, and long after we had seen through it Nora would give the expected cry of alarm just so as not to disappoint him. He would wink at me, as though to say, "Aren't women dear, simple creatures?"

And I would have to pretend to be gently indulgent to Nora. We used to laugh over it together afterwards.

One evening, though, we came into a field of Bob's with the young corn half-covered by the harrows, when he cried out in dismay "Why, they've nearly smothered the rows"; the very words that Nora had used in the previous field.

"But I thought it didn't matter," she said.

Bob disarranged his cap and scratched his head, quite red with chagrin. "But that was wheat—these are oats—and you mustn't cover oats. The devil," he kept muttering, stooping and smoothing away the earth from the tender shoots. "Never ought to have put a lad on to that job. Ruined the crop, I shouldn't be surprised."

However, the crop recovered.

This shows the amount of judgment the farmer relies upon his men to exercise, for the weather changes hourly and he cannot be all the time with them.

When a shower turns the rolling of corn from a beneficial to a harmful process—whether the harrows are merely loosening the earth about the roots of the corn or actually tearing them up—"doing too much to it," as they say. Or, maybe, they aren't going in deep enough at all, and a heavier set is necessary.

A lad has to learn, but the adult labourer would not continue harrowing with harrows that covered up the oats. His master might be away at market or a sale; he would take it upon himself to unhitch his horses and fetch a lighter set.

I have heard the men—the older ones particularly—expostulate with the master on some order being given them, through knowledge of the state of a field, one which the master may not have visited lately, but which lay perhaps against the labourer's back door, so that he knew it as well as his own garden. "We marn't take they heavy harrows on there, master;

they'll wholly play smash with they beans," he'd say, and all but refuse to execute what he considered a rash order. The good master, while often overriding the men's fears—(and they always err, the men, on the side of the over-cautious)—would nevertheless pay heed to what they say, and make a point of going to the field in question and seeing the harrows at work, whether the man were right or he.

That such personal pride in the work was not dead, though agriculture was for a while moribund, we would be reminded as we went for these evening walks. We found Bob's bearded barn-man, who also steered or went behind the corn-drill, lying on his back under the machine putting on some new coulters, which Bob had bought from Stambury only that afternoon, in order that the drilling should proceed efficiently next morning. He looked like a victim beneath the claw of some monster as he lay there in the earth, kicking this way and that as he wrenched at the nuts with a spanner. The drill was right out in fields burning with sunset, and his brown-ribbed corduroy trousers seemed to grow out of the soil. They were stiff and round as pipes and corrugated in sharp creases where he moved, as though he were jointed like a doll.

His name was Todd, and he was overseer of the barn. Bob's was a long barn with four porches, dated 1811 on one of its bricks. Here Todd dressed the corn that was for seed—here he thrashed beans with a flail in the autumn, because the machine was inclined to split them, which, of course, rendered them useless for planting—here he mixed vitriol with the seed-wheat to protect it from disease. Then he weighed it up and took it into the field all ready harrowed to receive it, laying the sacks at convenient intervals along the hedge. He would supervise the corn-drill, cleaning out of it every grain of the last seed (if of a different kind), setting the gear-wheels right and the weights and the cups (they have to be changed for almost all kinds of grain, according to their varying sizes). Lastly he would go behind it as it put in the seed, making himself responsible for those grains from the time he shovelled them out of the general heap till they vanished from sight into the earth.

Barn management is a craft in itself. No one outside a farm would imagine how easy it is for small quantities of different kinds of corn to accumulate in sacks—"left-overs" such as vitrioled wheat from drilling, a bushel of tares, a few pecks of clover seed ("gold dust" we used to call it in the days when it was worth twenty pounds a sack), "tail" corn from thrashing. It is so easy to say, "Leave them for now as they are." Next day they are forgotten, and when next one has to clear the barn for thrashing the corn pours out of every sack when shifted as through a sieve, for the mice have been living and multiplying on it in the meantime.

Charlie Todd's management of the barn was a kind of primitive domesticity. Bags that had held artificial manure were more prized by him than anyone—and it is wonderful how valuable far beyond their worth these are on a farm. The cry is always, "Is there an old bag about anywhere?"

These bags Charlie laid upon the barn-floor like mats, as well as keeping a bundle of rotten ones at the door for all to wipe their boots on before entering. He used to roll them and edge the heaps of corn with them, keeping the wheat and the barley and the beans and the peas all separate from one another.

On wet days Charlie would be particularly watchful, for if they got the chance the men would steal the bags to cover their heads and shoulders, or for aprons if they went hedging.

Charlie, like the old taskers in the days when all thrashing was done by flail, kept a special pair of nailless boots for wear in the barn, as these did not split the grains.

The two chief pieces of furniture were the dressing-machine and the scales and weights.

There was a wooden dais at one end, on either side of which the beams rose and curved ruggedly to the roof, some with the bark still on them; a small door opened from half-way up on one side, through which sheaves had once been pushed at harvest-time. I have seen the sun coming through this opening in a single shaft, striking down upon the dais, a sloping pillar of haze. One was aware suddenly of the emptiness of the place, and of a presage and concentration, as though light were mind. One waited for the first actor in some old play to enter and halt there and speak his prologue.

Then I looked again, and Charlie Todd stood in the gleam, not by chance either, but for it to light up the better the corn which he offered to me in each hand, saying, "Which will ye have, sir? Will ye choose which ye'd rather?" For I had come for seed-barley, and my horse and tumbril stood at the doors.

The doors—they in themselves detain my mind's eye. Four doors to each porch. The lower ones about as high as a man's shoulder; the upper ones lofty enough to admit the greatest load that human ingenuity could stack on the narrow base of a harvest wagon. A little droop-hinged with time, these last, a little slack, a little complaining now like old limbs at being moved. But what furious monsters they could become in a gale of wind! Then they rattled and moaned like a fettered man for freedom. To undo them was an occasion for such attitudes of caution as might be shown towards an uncertain beast. The fitful wind seemed to impart a craftiness. They would rest quiet as death in the taut grasp of Charlie Todd; then, his hand relaxing a moment, a rush of air would snatch them from him; they'd

swing back and crash crazedly against the barn wall.
I have seen Charlie pushing might and main to shut
one, and then brought to a halt midway by some more
vicious gust, and give back a pace or two, till others
came to add their weight to his.

But what a haven that barn seemed in such
tempestuous weather, when one heard one's voice,
still shouting, echo loudly in its roof, and the sudden
stillness was like a wave of heat to one's face. An
ark it was indeed, with all creation rushing madly
past the open doors, the sky crowding down and the
top of the straw-stack whirling up to meet it.

Charlie Todd was a treasurer; he looked like one;
he bore, as it were, the generous reflection of maturing
suns on his face. It was rosy and bronze, as though
fronting a light of harvest, an afterglow. His beard
too, as though with Midas's power, having touched the
brown corn, had taken its hue.

I have a picture of him looking up as I entered, that
moment of re-focused attention when his blue eyes
would light up with greeting, and his beard would
thrust towards me in a jolly, arrogant way, like the
rustic wit he cried out at me for conversation—his
talk was like the gleams of a racing sky lighting here
and there at random. But when he held some corn
up to the daylight in his shovel to examine it his beard
would lie upon his breast, and then he looked wise and
solemn.

Bob Chilgrove, his master, would walk in and say,
"We start thrashing to-morrow, Charlie—that stack
of wheat, those oats; barley and peas for seed."

Charlie would scan the stacks well, then turn back
into the barn whose roof seemed lit only by cobwebs
that spread themselves as though just to catch the grey
light, and piece out the space.

It had all to go somewhere and none to get mixed.
Unless he had it planned clearly in his head before-

hand there would be a muddle; for the machine was inexorable, pouring it out all day, and the men carrying it in, bent blindly with the loads, their eyes toward the ground. They could not think in the exhaustion of labour; they would ask where, and Charlie would point out to them, and they would go on pouring sack after sack out on that one spot which he must heap with his busy shovel and mound against the wall, ever repulsing the creeping tide of piled grain which tended to encroach more and more into the middle of the barn.

Having cleared the floor of all remnants of last thrashing, Charlie swept the whole floor with his soft broom, and found a company of hens waiting when he opened the lower doors to thrust it out, as though the farm-yard sensed what he was up to; the sweepings were a choice and varied feed for the poultry. Then he took hammer, nails, and pieces of tin (he never threw away a tin, but hammered it into sheets) and nailed them over any new rat-holes, tested every corner and crevice, for whole sacks of corn could pour away down any one.

Next he lowered the sacks from the cross-beam whence they had hung since last in use, to be away from mice. Every one he turned inside out so that there should be no grains already in them to get mixed with the new corn. Finally any holes he would cobble with sack-needle and string, sitting on the step of the dais like a tailor, chewing tobacco all the time. It was strictly forbidden to smoke in the barn—but tobacco he would have.

Then he was ready. Morning came. The engine hissed; the wheels began to turn. The barn-doors swung open and Charlie stood ready to receive the grain into the vast, proud, spruce interior, while the great cobwebs up in the roof stirred with the air of the doorway and swung to and fro like torn old banners.

THE CHERRY TREE

It was now that the holidaying school-children would make free of the lane that ran through our fields. Never a one would there be all winter, but women loading themselves with firewood after a storm, filling their aprons with fallen branches, or sacks which overburdened their backs when lifted. They were figures of stress with flying hair, working with grim and nervous energy, pausing to turn their grey faces to the grey sky a moment, then up with their loads, and their eyes to their feet all the squelchy way home. These always seemed to me the sorriest figures of the countryside, working at fury-pitch within the four walls of their cottages, their souls near-sighted with living from one job to another and little aware of the outside world. Their haunted eyes showed that Time —through children and poverty—was their pursuer, and their anxiety that they guessed they should be outstripped by him at the last.

I have heard their voices scolding, shrill, as I have passed by an open door, turning the black interior into a vortex. Yet from this vortex issued the unhurried, unharassed farm-worker, and children smiling and staring, absorbing every flower and wing-flutter into their growing life.

It was the turn of the year indeed when March winds slackened, scattering no more of this fuel-manna, and a softer air made it less of a need. Then the word would go round, just about the time that the whipping of tops came to an end in the school playground, that the primroses were out along Largess Lane; the children would come and people the place, drifting along the hedges, wandering away at sundown with suns of yellow posies in their hands.

Yet they never seemed to make any difference to the number of flowers that grew there.

Spring was delicate along our meadow hedges, and all the birds were in pairs except for knots of sparrows that rushed by, disputing madly. The occasional single partridge that one put up on one's walk seemed a sad thing somehow, betaking herself away with a cry up against a full-bosomed cloud.

It was on Good Friday that I noticed a bush of palm-willow had burst from its buds of silver-grey storm light into cocoons of soft gold — Titania's powder-puffs. It stood out of the hedge in the middle, surrounded by a bodyguard of briars, a graceful and rejoicing plume.

Bank Holiday would be unnoticed in the country here, were it not for townsfolk friends and relations that give the little station four miles distant the bustle of a suburban one on the following Tuesday between eight and nine. The labourer works as usual, but the people from the neighbouring towns, employed and unemployed, go walking, cycling, and coaching by.

On Tuesday the road at the end of the lane became as quiet as the lane itself again. We farmers avoided it during Bank Holiday as a river in spate, kept our carts and implements off it; on Tuesday its major traffic became again the chiming rib-roller, the tumbril, and the laden barrow.

The primroses seemed to have learnt not to grow up that end of the lane, and I was considering how great liberations of the city-pent passed over like a cloud that thundered but did not fall, when my eye was taken by a solitary tassel of soft gold high in the air. There was only one; the rest of the palm-willow was scarred white where the sprays had been pulled off. Its lone stem went up in cricked joints—at every joint there had been a spray, forming its symmetry—the bodyguard of briars was crushed down; but one last plume the wounded tree still held out of reach of covetous hands. All else budded and grew as before; only this more ethereal beauty had perished.

But I was soon out for destruction myself. The young rooks were already sitting out on the boughs by their nests, trying their wings and making fluttering flights. Rooks and farmers never really agree; less still, rooks and poultry-farmers. So Bob Chilgrove and I spent a morning underneath our elms with air-guns. Down came the young rooks, one after another. It could not be called cruelty unless to the parents, for the young birds seemed to have not the slightest apprehension of danger, though their brothers tumbled headlong from beside them. They had only to return to their nests to be safe; yet they stayed perched. One received a flick on the tail-feathers from one of the lead pellets, which nearly overbalanced him. Even this produced no sense of fear; he recovered and turned round on the bough as though for the purpose of presenting a better target. The parent birds, though, circled round and round, crying out continually in their dismay. It seemed to me that, although rooks are reputed to have a considerable degree of understanding among themselves, there could be no meaning communicable between old and young, otherwise assuredly the fledglings would have been infected with the parents' alarm.

Somehow in spring the village seems more cheery and bustling—before the doze of summer sets in from which it is only roused by the September gun and horn. The sweet-shop seems gayer, before the sun stares in too greedily and compels a drawing-down of blinds; it becomes, almost, a glinting trinket-shop. The butcher and the grocer seem more various. A sightless calf's head gasps that veal is in, and it takes the whole of Mr. Jolman's many-paned window to frame the pyramid of oranges, fiery reminder of marmalade time. I was asking Nora what she would like for a birthday present as we passed old Mrs. Bosker's, and she answered, quick as thought, "The whole joy of buying twopenny-worth of sweets from that window."

Knowing the drift of her meaning, I answered, "You might as well have asked me for the moon. But here you are, if these are any use." I drew from my pocket two worn pennies with Queen Victoria fading away like a ghost on them. "Or stay; I can do a little better." I substituted two new ones as bright as gold. But she shook her head. "You are too late, you know."

What has happened to the cottage sweet-shops of our childhood? We conferred about them and agreed that we had hardly come across one since those days, though each of us owned one in memory—Nora's in Somerset and mine in Oxfordshire. The old widow women had died, of course—"and the canary whose cage danced as he sang in the window." "In my case a cat," sad Nora, "that used to sit and watch (I thought) the sugar mice, or close its eyes at you as you stood outside in the sun."

And no one, of course, had carried them on. Mrs. Bosker's was surely the last one in the land. Geraniums stood on either side in raddled pots and a fern hung above.

There had been, we agreed, almost always some small impediment, a Rubicon, which, once you had crossed it, committed you to the great moment of the spending of your twopence. In my case the window had been surrounded by a small wooden paling as here, and one entered within the pale through a wicket which clicked to behind one by means of a weight on a chain. "To reach mine you had to cross a plank bridge over a little brook," Nora said. "That took a certain amount of courage; it was only four of my steps across, but it seemed a very long and narrow way when the brook was full and roared underneath. Funnily enough, one never minded on the way back."

There had been just room for two children to stand side by side within the paling of my shop; I could see myself standing there—a so much taller paling than Mrs. Bosker's, it seemed, I being so much smaller—tapping on one of the diamond window-panes with a penny, hardly able to concentrate on the sweets for the antics of the canary all of a bustle in its cage as though calling, "Come along—somebody here to buy. Shop, please! Shop! Shop! Shop!"

But I longed for a minute's delay, for though I had quite made up my mind before entering in at the gate what I intended to buy, here had the old dame got quite a number of new things displayed in the coloured-paper trays; very good value some of them seemed, too; and I was again in a flurry of indecision. What a yawning depth of coolness and silence seemed the parlour beyond! It was like looking into a deep well, where for reflected day-gleam stood a small window in the opposite wall, a single pane which was a glimpse of green grass-plot and orchard bough, beautiful as hopes unrealised.

Vaguely a white lace cap became apparent within, a momentary twinkle of spectacles, then a hand cut off short into the dimness by black mittens approached the window-latch, which it opened, and in place of the little vista was the lace-fronted bosom of the proprietress overawing me with its golden cross.

Twopence bought a great deal there—it was quite a complicated order in the days when sweets could be had four ounces for a penny. First, a farthing's worth of Liquorice All Sorts—much more dainty and festive than it sounds. Item, a farthing sugar-stick. Item, a halfpenny bar of chocolate. Then some of those button-shaped sweets with endearments on them that the prince in the fairy-tale might have used to aid him in his wooing—"Dear One," "My Heart's Delight," "Will You Be Mine?" Lastly, which should it be, five aniseed balls, two sugar mice, or a sherbet dip?

I am sure that one's character does not change inherently a jot. Those indecisions, those starts of reckless extravagance, those shrinkings into anxious parsimony, have been with me from then till yesterday. Sometimes one never paused before the wicket, but went straight in and blued a whole penny on sweets with wrappers on, only an ounce; and I felt the heady pleasure mastering the awe of rashness of one play-acting wealth. Luckily, we never, most of us, reach the peak of ambition nor exhaust the store of worldly illusion. Few and apart in frilly paper dishes lay this old dame's choicest morsels. Whipped cream walnuts. The chocolate coating was surmounted with a rich flourish, the very signature of extravagance. Each one of these cost three-halfpence.

One day the occasion would burst upon me more glorious than the first of spring, when joy should loosen the last shackles of constraint, and I should buy, break open, internally discover and eat a whipped cream walnut. It never did; and now, alas, a whipped cream walnut has lost its meaning.

So when Nora desired the whole pleasure of spending twopence at Mrs. Bosker's window she asked for something past our present powers. "Even if every stick of barley-sugar were fire amber."

But two children were passing and paused, clinging to the palings and gaping at the sun-gay show, conversing secretly in tones of wonder as we might do facing up at some stained cathedral window.

Nora accepted my proffered birthday present after all and spent it through these two. It was no good us attempting the wicket gate. They soon stood im-pounded, tapping on the window. It was opened to them and complicated business done. But before it closed again Mrs. Bosker hailed us with, "That's a reg'lar picture, now," pointing to the white dome of our blossoming cherry tree, seen with the strangeness of distance from here.

The children conferred, and a spokesman was deputed. He advanced and proffered a bag. "Please will you have one, ma'am?" We each took a bull's eye and walked homeward in silence, swollen-cheeked.

CHAPTER VIII

"Just when he was most needed, too," Walter said. I agreed, but that was not all my elegy, for he was a friend, too, and about the same age as I was (reckoning one year of his to three of mine) when we started ploughing this land together. Darkie, the steadier horse of the pair, died in the night. Walter came with the news on Sunday morning. The more deeply veiled the implication of the native's words the more serious you may expect it to be.

"Old Darkie ain't got a mite of gee-up in him this morning, master."

"Eh—what?"

"Do you come and see."

Round the corner of the horse-yard a hoof shone at me as no living hoof could rest a minute. His haunches were collapsed into the straw. His head, though, had caught upon the manger and was thrust up with the lips drawn back from the teeth as though afraid. One of his front legs was doubled beneath him, but the other was planted forward in that gallant curve as when a horse makes to rise from the ground.

But death had been too heavy a load; he had been unable to rise beneath it.

"See here, master." The leg that looked so supple was as stiff as a board. "He's been dead some while. I reckoned that'd do for him in the end, the farcy."

I suppose Darkie I should consider one of my first

88

mistakes, for he was a Shire horse, and Shire horses
are reckoned unsuitable for our Suffolk heavy land,
as the "feather," or hair that spreads round their hooves,
collects the clay. Darkie used to come home sometimes
swinging tassels of mud in bunches from every leg. I
was wisely advised to get rid of him and buy in his place
a Suffolk Punch. The Suffolk Punch has "clean legs,"
as his advocates say with some superiority. He is best,
certainly, on our land.

But Darkie was a mild and steady fellow. He could
be left with a cart without creeping away with it into
the ditch after choicer herbs than those at his feet.
The rattling of a water-cart behind him did not startle
him into a gallop. In all those ticklish jobs, such as
horse-hoeing, when you need above all a horse who
will walk neither stumbling nor nodding like the one
Hardy observed, nor yet devouring the earth with
ecstasy of being, but straight and steady, so that you
don't cut up all your corn with shares that should be
clearing the earth *between* the rows—in Darkie was our
trust. He received, I fear, more than his fair share of
work in consequence. After ploughing most of the
day he would get harnessed to a tumbril to fetch a
load of straw, while his more mettlesome companion—
Dewdrop—was sporting in the meadow. ("A reg'lar
old varmint, Dewdrop be, 'tween shafts.") But what
was one to do?

Certainly I did not feel disposed to part with him.
They notch up in mind, too, the occasions that have
been cheerful for not needing to wonder what he would
be up to next. Slow journeys to the mill when one
could look about one at the hedges and over them at
others' crops, instead of being all the while alert for
what meteor of modern travel should be upon us from
yonder corner. Times when the morning was all,
coupled with the half-conscious persuasion that one
was pretty expert at judging to a nicety with the reins.

Darkie never bothered to claim his share of the credit. This understanding between the blinkered head and me grew into a sentiment above use—how seldom we met eye to eye, I reflected, remembering the kindly, smoky lustre that had been frozen like pools overnight into this glazed stare.

Yes, I stuck on to Darkie, and hoped that mud would not beget in him what it notoriously does in "hairy-legged 'uns"—split heels and "grease." The more so that he had three white feet to one black, and for some reason "grease" is said not to infect white, but only black ones. But he took it, too, and in the black hind foot. "That fairly reek on't," Walter bluntly put it when there was no longer any doubt. Not that "grease" itself will kill, but the "farcy" that develops from it may. The spring and the autumn were Darkie's bad times. His leg would swell, and the swelling would travel up his leg. Then it would subside and he would go to work again and be in good trim all the summer. Walter gave him mysterious brews of herbs which he picked and dried. There is a homœopathic lore handed down from one generation of horse-keepers to another. There are remedies of which the ordinary man, the farmer even, never hears; horse-keepers are more jealous of their secrets than chefs of their recipes. I have heard but the merest rumour of them and been astounded, and would have said that along with the practice of greasing the rusty nail that scratched you they were superstitions, but for irrefutable evidence that they worked. These things will go on till tractors rule the fallow's brown waves. And then also the last ornament will go from the life of work, the last trimming-up of toil with tinkling bells and polished plates, and we will have to sit up all night eating the corn the machines grow lest they outstrip themselves with production.

In the autumn Darkie would get it again. This time

the swelling would reach his belly. "Allus at the rise and the fall of the leaf," Walter said.

Another spring and it moved onward along his belly, and we turned him into the orchard to fight his fight with it. He stood still all day, the leg slightly drawn up, as though thinking. It was the field of the cloth of gold with buttercups.

I would walk out in the evening and look at him and wonder. We would stand looking at each other while I smoked a pipe. He stood where he had stood most of the day, and I knew he was fighting his fight with it although he never moved.

The sun went down, and a little wind came and went like a third person who found he wasn't wanted, and a few of the blossoms of the cherry tree under which we stood would fall and lie on his back and stay there. He became just a shape in the dusk, a gaunt black shape with a mottle of pale petals on his back. Nora would call from the lit window, and then I would give his neck a pat for good night, and go in.

He was better if he could be kept moving, and at first I would walk him about the orchard at any spare moments. Round and round we'd go, and then in and out among the trees for a change, Darkie's head nodding at my shoulder as he plodded along just as though we were embarked on a far journey through eternal avenues, and not continually passing over the ground of a minute before.

But he became too stiff for that; it hurt him to walk. He'd strike out a few steps and then the halter rope would tighten in my hand. I'd turn back and see what his eyes said, and take off the halter from his head and let him stand.

After that we nursed him in the yard and continued to dose him, but the swelling continued to move along nearer towards his heart, and he died.

It was Sunday, but among that group of people

whose attendance on human and animal emergencies
holds them ready on all days alike, was the horse-
slaughterer. My car was temporarily out of order, so
I had to take a pedal-cycle which once had arrived all
black and brilliant for a youthful birthday, but now
lay in dark corners prepared to serve a need when hunted
out.

Instinctively I hurried, though there was no hurry.
Recollecting that, I went easy and saw again a road I
had not seen for many a day, having been upon it only
in a car for years. But now I saw every flower in every
cottage garden, and letting the shadow of the occasion
remain where Darkie lay, discovered a solace in my all
but silent motion. It is no bad thing in life, I think,
to let a hiatus of travel be a hiatus of mind.

The horse-slaughterer lived in a house like a red box
down a cinder drive. A board proclaimed his name
and trade, and a pair of cow's horns nailed to the post
above gave it a somehow diabolical emphasis.

Lugubrious sheds squatted inscrutably about the
rear of the brick house. I remembered then how often
I had driven that way in a gig with Mr. Colville in the
days just after the war, when motors were both scarce
and dear, and how the horse would always veer to the
far side of the road and pass this establishment at a
canter. "He can smell the blood," Mr. Colville had
said to me.

The proprietor, however, was cheerful as a boy on
holiday—round-faced, with the conventional Sunday
black upon him certainly, but collarless, with trousers
many times rolled up and sleeves turned back, which
suggested that the Sabbath toilet would be completed if
and when circumstances might allow.

He was not surprised to see me. "I'd heard your
Darkie horse were wonderful bad again," he said.

He soon harnessed his own, which should have been
a Prince of Sorrows, and put it in his cart. My cycle I

found had a puncture, so at his suggestion I loaded it in among his winching apparatus and took the seat beside him. Not that I liked his cart. Homeward the view was less fair.

The business of getting the stiff-cold Darkie into the cart was grotesque—the dumb resistance of inertia approximated for a moment to the vivid obstinacy of the unbroken colt. But enough of that. One hoof was all that showed eventually from the humped cloth, though the very shape of the load was suspiciously unnatural for a Sunday morning. Walter and I watched it swing away down the road, the hoof with its yet bright shoe jerking an awkward farewell to us.

Of course, I ought to have bought a steady horse of that maturity labelled "aged" in sales catalogues to fill the gap. That was what I wanted, Bob Chilgrove assured me, to go between shafts, and I agreed with him. Perhaps if it hadn't rained so hard and con-tinuously at the sale I went to, I might have taken more interest in those that were paraded past, trotting from one whip-crack to another. They were cheap enough too. "Good old-fashioned sort," Bob would mutter through the shower from his hat-brim; and I would make some excuse or other. The auctioneer did his best to keep things lively with "Just let's see her trot again." And when this was accomplished with shouts and chasings and crackings of the whip, as though the white-coated attendants were celebrating some lively pagan festival, he'd cry, "See how she moves, gentlemen, see how she moves."

But I had no heart to bid for the weary old things. What with the state of farming, they changed masters almost every year nowadays. What was there to compare with the joy of working a young horse you had broken in yourself, and had known from the time it ran free and wild in the meadow?

I had long coveted, and long sought an excuse to
bid Bob Chilgrove for, one of his Suffolk colts. Their
long manes streamed in the wind as they cantered
about his meadows in their gusty humours. I do not
know of any view more delightful to the farmer's eye
than a batch of eight such colts as Bob saw from his
sitting-room windows, their coats yet unrubbed by
chain or thong, no mark of collar on their necks nor
bridle on their heads. Their tails were so long they
seemed to whisk the ground as they moved. There
they abode in freedom and grace, as though for the
picture that they made of the meadow. One hardly
noticed them alter, because every year Bob bred a foal
or two, and every year one or two of the colts were
broken in, and one or two old horses sold.

But, times being what they were, Bob admitted he
had too many, though he did not take active steps to
get rid of them.

"Will you have a deal with me for one of those?" I
asked. Bob again assured me that what I really needed
was a steady old horse, to his way of thinking, seeing
that Dewdrop wasn't "a mucher" in shafts. But what
I needed was not what I wanted. "I'd rather have
something that'll grow to be worth more than less,"
was the way I put it.

"Well, let's come and have a look at them," he
said, and we went out with our sticks and the comfortable intention of spending most of the morning
gazing at them from every possible angle, individually
and collectively, "seeing them move" (and these *could*
move), and gossiping on a variety of subjects as each
considered whether it were yet possible to advance or
drop his price another ten shillings. All this was
included in the phrase "having a deal."

First to spot your horse. (No, first to get the dog
from among them and send him home. He had followed
us out into the field, and now, relying on his greater

agility, was playing the toreador, barking at their heels, and, as these kicked empty air, appearing suddenly in front of them and making feints at their heads.) Next to spot your choice and identify him to his owner.

"That one with the white foot."

"I see, the white hind foot."

"No, the white front foot."

"That one in front of the rest."

"No, he's second as they're going now."

"Ah, but he was in front just then."

"That's the one."

"I see him—he's the best of them."

"Of course, you would say that!"

"Well, look at the bone, man! He came out of that Blossom mare of mine. I didn't really mean to sell him. Do you know, the stallion he was by——"

Here follows a history of the antecedents of the colt; he and his brethren all the while continue to stand and stare at us, coming nearer and nearer like curious aborigines, till the fact of Bob taking out his handkerchief to blow his nose sends them rearing backwards and galloping away, each infecting the other with hilarious pretence of alarm. Round and round us they canter, just as though we have them on an invisible trace. Then they pretend to no further interest, and go into the far corner and start feeding, stretching down their long fine necks just bulking into strength, as though with meekness, to the turf. For they are past their first gawkiness, and are not yet grown to the size and stolidity of labour. They are at their brief halcyon during which strength is composed in lines of grace; their wildness has a relation with the clouds. One stoops to drink in the pond by the hedge. He startles a blackbird from it, who in turn startles him, and he splashes up sudden wings of spray. That sets them all off, till they stop dead ten yards from us, and begin advancing step by step, all inquisitiveness again.

Proud creatures; yet their apprehensions are those of blown leaves on an uncertain day.

I notice something. "That one, third from last, seems to me to himp a bit."

"Which? The one with the tick of silver?"

"No, the one with the white forehead."

"Himp, do he?"

Several minutes of concentrated attention to discover whether he "himps" or not.

"Dammit, I believe you're right. Looks to me as though he's been kicked on the stifle."

We walk to the gate, and there Bob shouts across the yard, "Barrow."

"Barrow," the many walls echo.

"Barrow!"

"Coming, sir." The foreman comes rolling his squat figure along like an old tub boat.

"That colt there himp."

"Himp, do he?"

"Yes, he himp a tidy bit."

"I never knew on't."

"Well, you'd better catch him and get a hempen halter on him and see what's the matter with him."

Barrow retires, and we hear him complaining to the yard-boy, "How do he think anybody's going to catch one of they? Wild as witchery they be."

But we return and resume our business.

"Seventeen pounds, you said."

"Seventeen—— Hi! no, wait—I said seventeen-ten." (Nearly caught him napping that time.)

"Sixteen's my limit."

He shakes his head, and for the fifth time says, "Horses are getting scarce, you know. Hardly any foals have been bred for a long time. He's worth seventeen-ten if he's worth tenpence."

Impasse. My eyes loiter on the horizon as though they have done with horses. A faint whiteness over there.

"What's that? White clover?"

"Yes—looks like being a decent bit."

"Whose—Harper's?"

"Yes."

"Doing pretty well up there, isn't he?"

"He made a rare splash when he went in—new implements and everything."

"Money no object, seemingly."

"I don't know—I haven't seen any yet for seed-wheat he had off me last autumn."

"You'd better call round when he's sold his white clover seed."

"I reckon so. . . . Well, sixteen-ten, you said?"

"That's my limit—— Hi! no, what are you talking about? I said sixteen." (Nearly caught me napping that time!)

We carry on tentative deals over three of the colts simultaneously. It is like playing three games of chess at once. I advance my price: he lowers his. The gap diminishes.

In the end we clasped hands dramatically in the middle of the meadow, which is the proper way of clinching a deal, having come to terms over the one of my choice at sixteen-fifteen, and then walked briskly towards the house, conscious of having earned some refreshment.

My colt was a chestnut, but his mane and his tail were sand-coloured. When Walter and I went to fetch him, Barrow saw to it that he was there also, that we could help him catch the one that "himped." One of Walter's good points was that he had not the slightest nervousness of horses, whereas Barrow had considerable apprehensions, especially of colts. This showed itself in the ways the two men behaved with them. Walter seldom raised his voice, was calm and slow towards them. Barrow, though, sounded very· masterful the way he would shout "Gee! Woa! Come over there!

Hold up!" Actually he was but forestalling his fears that the horse was going to act contrary to his wish, which, of course, made the horse think it *was* doing something wrong; it became nervous and flustered—became, in fact, the very horse of his apprehensions.

Bob admitted his foreman was no hand with horses. "But he's a rare good chap with pigs." This was so. Bob Chilgrove's pigs always did well. Walter, on the other hand, managed them awkwardly, would always be giving them either too much or too little food, gave the sows too much straw to farrow in so that they lay on the pigs, and regarded the stud boar I kept as a devil out of hell. But the creature Walter really did fear was the honey-bee.

We approached the colts, and soon had them penned in a corner of the meadow—Walter, Barrow, the yard-boy, and myself. They stood shining the whites of their eyes at us and quivering. The interesting surmise then was, at whom would they make their dash to break through our cordon? For that was their immediate intention.

They rushed between Walter and me, startled by a threatening-nervous gesture from Barrow, who thought they were coming at him. All the time he had been keeping up a complaint. "We shall never catch they—wild as hawks they be—we shall never catch they, not if we chase about arter 'em all day," in that tone of defeatism which the labourer sometimes adopts in face of a job for which either he sees no need or has no stomach. At first this used to drive me to fury and despair, until I found that the man continued at the job nevertheless with unremitting perseverance until it was accomplished. But he would never cease announcing its impossibility until silenced by the ultimate success of his own dexterity. Even then, if you challenged him about it, he would assure you that but for some coincidence quite outside his control it would never have been done.

Next time we split the colts. Five and three—and two out of those three were the ones we wanted. Then Walter, who had said hardly anything so far, took command.

"Do you keep they others back," he said, and we turned and kept the five others at a distance, leaving Walter alóne before the three, standing before them on a narrow piece of ground between the fence and the pond. He wanted to do it in his own way, before Barrow's hurly-burly had frightened the colts. So we left him to it. Either they must give themselves to him, or knock him down to go past him, the place where he stood being very narrow.

For a long time he seemed to do nothing, standing there with the halter in his hand, looking about him. He stood carelessly, murmuring, "K-p, k-p, k-p k-p," in a soft falsetto. The neighing of the others alarmed the three, who made a rush towards. him, but he never moved, and they stopped and wheeled away.

Then suddenly as from nothing he ducked, swore, ran back. "Blast the bloody old bee!" cried he whom wild horses could not stir.

The bee passed. He stood and waited by the pond. The soft noise in his throat kept the colts' ears a-quiver. They were impelled towards it. They came and sniffed deeply of his clothés, of the back of his hand. He patted a neck; his arm crept under and up and round. His fingers were tightly twisted into the thick, sand-coloured mane. Next moment the halter was on the one and on the other. The third followed mildly behind, till the neighing approach of the others broke the spell, and it galloped away to them.

For the first time the other two realised they were prisoners. It was a drunken, struggling exit we made from that meadow. I held my colt while Walter ran to help Barrow with his, which had nearly escaped him. It was like wrestling with a wave which reared and impended over me.

All the way home to Silver Ley he kept turning his wild head to whinny and listen for the answer which came from the others, fainter and yet fainter.

When he stood locked in the yard at Silver Ley he neighed and listened, and could hear no answer. And again he neighed and listened, and there was nothing but the wind. He stood with his head raised in sharp suspense, "afraid as a grasshopper."

After a day or two we began breaking him in. First we put the bridle and harness on him. The blinkers quenched the quick challenge of his eyes. They stilled his head and narrowly confined him. The harness lay on him awkwardly; his whole body by its fleet shape somehow repudiated the strappings that were to look natural on him for the rest of his life.

He stood in the yard a whole morning. Sometimes he gave a spasmodic jump into the air, as though to shake the harness from him; sometimes he tried to rub it off against a post. But for the most part he just stood miserably still, as though trapped between two narrow walls by the blinkers.

Then Walter took him out on the meadow, driving him on a long rope for reins. The turf beneath his feet seemed to rouse him, and he kicked up his heels and started to gallop off home. The rope was long, but not long enough for that. It tautened with a jerk that made him rear, swinging Walter round as he crouched on it at the other end.

He dragged us both with slithering feet a little way.

For two hours Walter played him like a huge fish. It was a contest of man's patience against his fine young lust for freedom.

Gradually he ceased to plunge, to start away, but trotted round and round Walter on the rope. Already his sporadic force was being bent to a more regular course.

The work exhilarated Walter. He called out to him in a voice full of good cheer, "Walk up, Boxer! Gee, Daylight, come along, my old dear." The very moulding of the colt's will to his own seemed to bring the two into a kind of kinship. Walter was very pleased with the colt; he had wanted no old horse either. Barrow, now, would have welcomed one.

I ever marvel at what a medley lies in the deeps of the labourer's mind, which at any moment may be surprised to the surface. The colt was not yet named; but Walter had an exuberant vocabulary which he sang out in the delight of his mastering occupation. "Woa, Rapid! Woa, London-After-Dark! Gee, then, Jack-in-the-Box. Steady, Timbertoes."

Next we made him drag a log of wood. He refused, backed on to it, then tried to gallop in fright away from it. We all ran full speed round the meadow. "I can keep it up as long as he can," Walter cried, laughing and panting. He soon tired, and stood with heaving flanks and peony nostril. The harness had branded his peerless coat already with the marks of toil.

He sulked awhile, standing awkward as a lump of wood himself. Walter waited. Soon he learned that the freedom of impulse was for him no more, that mysterious shackles bound him to a voice which commanded not speed, but plodding power. He obeyed, stepping it out with submissive grace that itself became a sort of pride, the fleetness of his young neck arched in quiet effort, his long fair tail floating like a pennon, as he dragged the stiff crass log.

I said to Nora, as she came out and we watched together this harmonious victory—the oldest in the world of man over beast—"We must give him a name, or Lord knows what Walter will be calling him next."

"Gee, then, Captain Cuttle," cried Walter. (I marvelled at the agility of his sixty years against the colt's young strength.)

"There you are, then," said Nora.

"What—Cuttle?"

"No, Captain."

So, having conquered him, we called him Captain.

There was another addition to our stable about this time which should have been mentioned before. A certain Jerry Hogbin, who was a higgler and rough dealer living mostly, as far as I could gather, on the awe-inspiring effects of his blustering voice, paid me a visit. He was a large man, but he drove up in the back of a tub-cart slightly bigger than a pram drawn by a dutiful, dumpy little pony. "Woa!" he cried, and the pony for very zeal not only stopped but backed a pace or two. His load, miraculously balanced, converted the cart into a kind of travelling tower— three hen-crates, a quantity of old motor-tyres, a hutch of rabbits, a box of eggs, on top of this two bags of chaff (his perquisite for "having a deal" with a farmer), and on them Jerry himself. The pony seemed glad of the rest. He was still six miles from home.

Now, I have heard people living in towns complain of English eggs. "We would like to be patriotic," they say, "but not only are home-produced eggs dearer, but also often less fresh than foreign ones." Sadly I had to concur; for observe the eggs in Jerry's box. He has just bought them from cottagers who keep a dozen hens each, so some of them are already a week old. He will take them to market next Tuesday; but if he thinks eggs are on the rise and he might get a better price, he will buy them in again, and try them in another market on Thursday, and again maybe on Saturday, and so on presumably until they explode with rottenness. They have still to pass through the wholesale

merchant's hands and get to the shop, where they must
wait until you come in and buy a dozen.

Steps are at last being taken to save the scientific
poultry industry from the bad odour with which Jerry's
eggs have been infecting it by grading, testing, and
stamping. Not a day too soon.

"Have you got anything to sell, master?" Jerry
cried as usual, and as usual I shook my head. An
occasional deal with old hens had encouraged him, and
he was persistence itself. It was quite difficult not to
get entangled in a haggling match with him.

"Nice-looking cockerels over in the meadow there.
What do you reckon they're worth?" But I would
not give an opinion, knowing he'd use it as a jumping-off
ground.

He tried again. "What about that old horse in the
orchard?" Darkie stood there at the beginning of his
last attack of farcy. "He ain't no good to you."

"Maybe not," I said.

"I'll take him off your hands for you."

I shook my head.

"I'll give you a couple of quid for him—there."
He leaned back on his chaff-bag throne with an air of
generosity.

"No—but I'll tell you what I'll do," I said. "I'll
give you that for yours."

"What—my pony?"

"And harness and trap."

"Oh, the whole turn-out," he grandiloquently called
it. "No, dammit, you know that ain't enough."

"Will you sell it?"

"Sell anything!" bawled Jerry, leaping down agog
for a good haggle. It was the motto of his life. "Sell
you the coat off me back, if you like"; and he half
peeled it from his shoulders to demonstrate his readiness.
But I didn't want his coat.

The pony was pot-bellied with poor feeding, but

sound enough. I wanted a rough outfit like that for carting food to the poultry. After long leaning on the gate with him, I bought the lot for three pounds. With more oats and less chaff and a cribful of sweet hay, Kitty soon began to take an interest in life again; for at first she seemed to have had none. The trap, with a little polishing up, was quite presentable. For though it had been bought primarily for rough work, at the moment we were very glad of it as a conveyance, our car having broken its axle. I had given it every chance of being a good, trusty little car, and it had tried my patience hard. Now at last I knew that it was a rotten little car without doubt, and would go on letting us down for the rest of its life. In the meantime Kitty took us about very pleasantly and confidently. The argument of winter being absent, it appeared to us that motoring with its attendant mechanical apprehensions could not stand up against care-free travel such as this. We discovered the old twisting by-roads to our little towns, whose flinty surfaces deterred all cars, and became quite friendly with them. It was years since I had heard the crunch of iron tyres on a stone road, and it awakened memories of my first days in agriculture. To people who said, "Yes, but one loses such a lot of time getting from place to place," we answered, how could that time be lost which was enjoyed?

(It was an American who said to the stranger, "Let's go by the new subway—it saves a whole minute." And the stranger was from the Orient who replied, "And what shall we then do with the minute?")

Driving a pony and trap one's eyes are released from the road hypnotism of motor travel; one gazes upon the fields and up into the trees. Gardens present themselves like Nature's shop-windows, and domestic moments through open cottage doors. The birds are not frightened from the hedges; paddocked horses look over and greet the stranger. If you are alone, you

have that jogging head in front to talk to—Kitty is
company; and if you are two, then she is a shadowy
third—a silent intimate. It is not merely the handling
of reins instead of wheel; one slips into another rhythm
of life altogether, as different from the mechanical as
the regular jog of the trap is from the jumpy reper-
cussions of the car on the roadway. One's radius
both contracts and expands. That is to say, while the
circumference of miles at one's disposal is halved, their
content is more than doubled. For quiet pace is like
a magnifying-glass; regions one has before passed over
as familiar suddenly enlarge with innumerable new
details and become a feast of contemplation.

In our little shopping town our pony and trap procured for us all unexpectedly this forgotten courtesy—
that the grocer came out to us in his fretted apron
and took Nora's order over the wheel. It gave quite
a new charm to our conception of the town. The
grocer by his simple act (hourly performed years ago)
attained in our eyes the dignity of a host. We felt that
a horse and trap were the only right conveyance in which
to thread that old street, seeing that the street so
honoured it.

We took Kitty everywhere—the worse the road the
better—and found we had been living in an undiscovered
country. The quiet of such travel was itself restful
after the rattle of the only degree of car that we could
afford. We bought ourselves a great green gig umbrella,
which covered the whole of our diminutive vehicle
like a palanquin when it rained. It sounds absurd, I
suppose, and probably looked so, but we enjoyed it,
and hardly felt the lack of a wider range. I suppose
we shall grow "dunt," as they say, when we grow o d,
and gape and shake our heads when strangers ask us
the way, being so locally minded. But then, Fancy
cannot be both at home and abroad. One can only
take one bite of life, whether one nibble at every land

105

or explore thoroughly a single parish. There are still people in ours who can neither read nor write, *but*— they aren't the slowest witted.

The motor-expert's report on our car was that it would be a twelve-pound job. But his twelve-pound look was as dismal as if the money were to come out of his own pocket. I soon understood it though, because, after acting undertaker's mute over the thing for a minute he said, "You know the car ain't hardly worth it—it'd pay you to get a new one. I could allow you a little for this." That would cost, he estimated, about a hundred and fifty pounds. "Yes, you could get a good, reliable car for that." "I don't believe there is such a thing," I said, which shocked him more than blasphemy—much—for without the potentially perfect piece of mechanism—the Very Car of Very Cars—his life would have had no co-ordinating purpose.

I asked Nora whether she would like us to spend a hundred and fifty pounds of our money on a reliable means of mechanical transport, and she replied that it appeared a dreadful lot—not for a car, but for the convenience of getting from one place to another when our actual needs to do so were so few.

"Even twelve pounds," she said, "seems too much." She asked, "I suppose we can't go on as we are?"

"Well, nobody does, do they? I mean, living five miles from a town with only a pony and trap is to-day conventionally intolerable."

"But I *have* enjoyed our drives."

"So have I," I said, but I would not influence her one way or the other.

"Would you awfully miss it——" she began, but I interposed, "It is you who should miss it."

"Yes." She thought about it. "But I don't," she brought out finally. "I haven't missed it at all these months; have you?"

"On the contrary, I should rather miss not sitting behind Kitty."

"Then let's go on as we are," we agreed. I went out to the waiting motor-man who clearly expected capitulation over the hundred and fifty pounds, and answered his ultimatum with another. He could buy my car; I was not going to buy his.

Oh dear, no, he was not going to do that. He flung away with a burst of refusal. But he turned back. "But then you'd have nothing—you can't live in a place like this without a car."

"But we can—we do."

He shrugged. "Well, that thing's no use to me or anybody."

"Oh, yes," I corrected. "I can turn it into a hen-house."

To save any mechanical thing, perhaps, from such insult he gave me three pounds for it, and departed quite overburdened with gloom at our apostasy to the modern definition of "Necessity."

CHAPTER IX

BEES are a gift of the air, coming to hang like a monstrous fruit under the blossoms of May. Of all who keep bees and belong to that devoted brotherhood of hive-watchers, how many have not started fortuitously by the arrival of a swarm about their heads, literally "out of the blue"?

That was how it happened to us. It was a Saturday afternoon. The week's work on the farm was over—the horses grazed in the meadow; pigs were littered with straw; mangolds had been ground for the cattle; and now, after lunch, my pocket-book depleted with paying wages but my heart light, I composed myself in a chair in the sun to the full rich idleness of the labouring man till tea-time.

But hark! A growing murmur in the old cherry tree; a million motes were zigzagging in the clear air above me. I stirred hastily to escape the visitation, but even as I did so I saw a black wen big as my fist on the underside of a bough, and was held fascinated, watching it grow, while the murmur died away above. On the face of it it looked an impossibility, a flouting of the laws of gravitation, but there the bees all hung in the shape of a bunch of grapes, tapering, pendulous, swaying slightly with the bough, a creeping, shimmering multitude each supporting and supported by his fellows.

How was it that the queen and her immediate hangers-on were not smothered? How did they bear the weight

of all the rest and not lose hold of the bough? Such
questions were undertones of wonder to a mercenary
jingle that kept running in my head:

> A swarm in May
> Is worth a load of hay.

I saw, with an uncomfortable conscience, the ghost
of the aged man who had acquainted me with that
rhyme, admonishing my inertia with it and pointing
his stick at the swarm.

"They'll stay there awhile," I thought, moving my
chair; "till next morning, probably."

"Not when the sun shines so warm," the shade
answered.

"In any case I've no hive."

"A box would do—to make shift."

I sat and watched while the inward debate went on,
and a vague compulsion grew against my natural indolence and timidity.

Just as I rose up determined to do something the
swarm dissolved away into the air again, and the postman came along the garden path with a telegram.
The telegram I was expecting, and I knew its contents
—the bees engaged both our attentions, booming away
to the meadow in a shadowy skein. When I say
"postman," I mean postman rather by accident of
uniform. Intrinsically he was a visionary-looking old
countryman. His garden was templed with a few straw
bee-skeps.

"Have you a tin can and a key?" he asked breathlessly.

"What for?"

"Quick, or they'll be gone," he commanded; so I
rushed in, seized a frying-pan from my astonished
wife's grasp, pulled the great key from the back-door
lock, and thrust them at him. He immediately began
beating the one upon the other and ran off after the

bees. I followed as far as the top meadow, where I
had a view of him with his face raised to the sky stumbling over clod and furrow, through hedges, over ditches,
and away, away, never ceasing his tattoo. Even when
he was out of sight I still heard his ting-ting-ting faintly
through the idle afternoon like some ancient tocsin of
alarm. Any week-ender who might have met the
postman rushing about the fields with those domestic
implements must have wondered at the frenzies indigenous to village life. It seemed a long time before he
returned, dishevelled and broiled in his thick serge
uniform—but without the bees, or knowledge of their
whereabouts. This tintinnabulation of his was supposed to be a specific against an escaping swarm,
causing it immediately to settle. But the magic hadn't
worked—not for the first time, I expect, though
nothing apparently could shake his faith in it.

I recompensed him with beer for his zealous, if unavailing, performance, and being refreshed he went on
his way.

The next morning, which was Sunday, there came
to me a man from the next village, of about the same
age as the postman, but with an eye as keen as the
other's was bemused and superstitious. His square,
black Sabbath suit misfitted him with a peculiar dignity.
He'd heard, he said, as how I'd lost a swarm.

Well, yes, I answered, in a sense, if its hanging for
an hour from my cherry tree constituted that I'd ever
had it.

It had settled, he said, on one of his bushes, and
he'd "taken" it in a box, and there it was waiting for
me if I'd care to carry it home.

I thanked him, telling him also, as though to put a
little more claim to it, how our postman had chased it
throughout the latter part of yesterday afternoon,
making a noise to it by striking a key upon a frying-
pan.

Whereupon his lean face grizzled up in contemptuous laughter, hollowing his keen eyes yet deeper in under his brow.

"He might just as well try to catch a bird by putting salt on its tail," he said.

I had heard of this man, though I had not met him before. His name was John Pready, and I had heard that he had been a shoemaker, and knew something about bees.

So I went along with him, and from his conversation it soon became apparent that he was to the postman what science is to superstition. He was old and bent, dry as a withe unbound from a twelve-month faggot, but by dint of making his legs very busy he walked very quickly, so that I had to stir mine, that usually go in a pacing, indolent fashion, to keep up with him. When I came to his plot of land—which was not far across the fields—I found a number of modern hives ranged under the hedge, newly painted white miniature chalets, overlooking the foot-high forest of his clover crop.

The swarm which was "mine" was contained in an inverted box on a board with two pieces of stick keeping a gap at one edge, between which bees kept taking the air and alighting.

One's first swarm is apt to seem rather an embarrassment at first sight. Mine did, particularly as my guide initiated me into the craft amid the maze of aerial traffic of the hives, and my attention was taken up in dodging his bees—of which he took no notice whatever—rather than in laying up his directions about mine.

He talked a long time among the hives, absentmindedly brushing a bee from the back of his hand or his coat every now and then. He told me what to do with the swarm and how it would increase, and of what absorbing interest I should find bee-keeping to become. Not least, he tried to dispel any fears I might have shown as to the main lay notion of bees—their desire to sting. They were really gentle, peaceable creatures, he said, and only stung as a last resort.

"But," he warned me, "they take a dislike to anyone smelling of drink." This was a disappointment, as bees are mostly a hot-weather job, and there is no refreshment, I think, like a glass of beer.

"Now, you'll need a hive," he said.

I suggested (with a mental view of the postman's garden) a straw skep, as being both cheap and traditional, but he condemned this idea utterly as false economy, for with a skep you have to smoke the swarm to death to take the honey—which is even then of very poor quality owing to the brood being mixed up in it. A modern hive, on the other hand, allowed of free manipulation from above, and of taking the honey with little disturbance to the tenants—and what pure, clear honey! Did I not know those squares of comb honey, so expensive and so beautiful on the breakfast-table? These were easily obtainable from the modern hive, he told me. At that I agreed to the extra outlay, and his disappointment at my suggestion out of the dark ages after his highly technical instructions was appeased.

He made hives, he said, and could provide me with one at a third less than they would charge me at a shop. In fact, he happened to have one by him all ready painted, if I'd care to see it.

He took me round behind a shed, and there one glistened in the sun, a white, Lilliputian palace.

I took it home on my shoulder, complete with all its interior furnishings—which was a sufficient load for one person over fields—and set it in the orchard and arranged its storeys.

Admittedly this was Sunday, but, though it is blasphemy to meddle in arable activities on that day, it is proper to tend one's livestock, and no sin to hive a swarm, particularly in the evening when the Sabbath calm begins to wear a little thin.

So I returned to John Pready in the evening as he had instructed. He wore his daily coat over his Sunday trousers and was waiting by the swarm. Very gently he took the sticks from beneath the box and lowered it on to the board. As it touched, the swarm inside gave a sharp "Z-zz!" as much as to say, "Ho! there, what are you up to?"

Then he swathed the whole thing in a white cloth and knotted the top, as though it were a pudding. And so, lifting it, board and all, he started off, I following with certain paraphernalia, till we reached the orchard.

The hive entrance was regulated by sliding shutters. We opened the portals their widest, laid a board sloping up to them from the ground, having first spread a white cloth there lest any should fall and perish in the forest of grass. I must mow the grass, he said.

He lifted the box and showed me the swarm sleeping suspended in a lump from the roof. Then he jerked it violently on to the board, where it shattered into a black bewildered horde creeping in all directions. But taking the smoker from my hands he puffed them into unanimity. They turned and marched up the slope like an army of slaves dragging a single block to the building of the pyramids. I found a sense of power out of proportion to their size and mass in watching them, as in men all at one purpose. And men, when they work in unanimous myriads like that, are no more than this multitude of bees, crawling on the face of the earth, building up they know not why. Only the individual is transcendent, sitting aloof with his faculties balanced and true to him, his instinct seeking the stars for touchstone, or sitting alone in his garden enjoying the godhead of observation of hurried lesser life.

Thus was my first swarm hived; and whenever in after-life this subject of bees recurs I am flashed back to that dusk—it is the little play for ever acted in the scene of "summer evening," when stillness endows the lightest leaf with a quality of endurance transcending its nature—a fixity as of iron wrought with art.

And again in the broad day—still in the thick and fretted scene of summer, I see myself and John Pready wearing that hermaphrodite garb of veil, white gloves, straw hats (Pready wore an old one of his wife's), and trousers tied at the boots, which somehow seemed to connect us with Morris dancers and the robust yet beribboned masquerade of antique joy. We bore in the oozing combs, while the orchard shade was all a-murmur round us. The kitchen reeked of sweetness while we extracted the honey and put it into pots; and afterwards, when at last the table was cleared, we sat and had tea, John Pready, Nora, and I, with some of the new honey in a brown bowl, on the flavour of which John would give his opinion, whether it were clover-honey, or willow-honey, or ivy-honey, or what.

For my single hive in a year or two had increased to six, and I graduated from John's scholar to his colleague, and we would meet and chat about our hives as two kings might discuss their subjects—how some were orderly and loyal, while others were malcontents and openly hostile to our will. Like Pharaoh, we stored during plenty against famine and provided for our peoples.

Nor was our state without enemies. The yellow peril was as real to us as to the greater world; for the wasps would descend in sudden hordes to kill and plunder. Many fierce battles have been fought at the portals of the hives, leaving the ground thick with dead.

John had a dozen hives in all, but these represented

merely his tenacity of purpose, not the sum of his experience. For he would tell us of his life as we sat at tea in our farm kitchen, how he had started as a village shoemaker as his father had been, the top of whose head bent over his work used to be regarded almost as part of the bay window of his shop to those who passed by—which turned from black to white in that position in course of time, to be replaced at last by the red-haired pate of his son. He used to make the best pair of boots for fifteen shillings obtainable hereabouts, Walter assured me, a pair which, if regularly greased, would keep out the wet for twelve months. Seeing that the labourer is walking all winter in a saturated dough of clay, and all summer first through dew-drenched meadow, then over rock-baked fallow, that speaks well for a pair of boots.

But whether one generation of crumpling of the chest over work was visited on the next or not, John Pready, while yet young, fell into a decline, and was told by the doctor that if he would save his life he must live it in the open air. But what shall it profit a man if he save his life and lose his livelihood? was the question that haunted him as he sat in the healing sun one day in May. Whereat the air grew murmurous as though in answer, and bees flew down from the sky through a space between the apple trees, and swarmed upon a currant bush close before him.

From that swarm he built up a colony of a hundred hives, and engaged in all the business that experts engage in—sending hives to the moors when the heather was in bloom, selling queens, swarms, and supplying a large London store regularly with the bulk of his honey. He showed me a photograph—now sallow and shiny—of his larger field regimented with hives like a municipal housing scheme, and himself in the middle, wearing the straw hat and white ducks which are the beekeeper's uniform and make him a figure of optimism in our preponderantly grey and boisterous calendar.

That was his zenith. Disease was reported from the Isle of Wight, and year by year John Pready found it spreading closer about his East Anglian retreat. It came at last, and left every hive dead and silent to the clarion sun of May.

Everything had to be destroyed. When he had burnt all his hives he farmed his land as a smallholder for a few years. Then, one day, he found a swarm hanging from the handle of his plough as he led his horses out after dinner. He tied up his horses at a safe distance, took it, and started to build up his colony of bees again.

Now he had twelve hives. For, like a bee himself, he was patient and blindly pertinacious. All summer he would be swinging his long scythe—stooping low over it—mowing the grass in front of his hives, that it should not impede their coming and going. Did he ever once straighten himself and look over to the horizon? I don't think so. He was like a man looking through a microscope; his vistas were all an intensification of the minute, as he manipulated his doll's houses of hives, floor by floor, sometimes piling storey upon storey till there were sky-scrapers in Lilliput, driving his fingers sometimes to the very ultimate sanctuary of the community, the royal boudoir—cutting out queen cells to prevent swarming. That was ever his preoccupation in the spring, to stop these lyric, these wasteful love-flights, to keep them to the task of honey, honey, honey. A jealous god.

His maxim was "Take time by the forelock." He was always coming out with it. It was the watchword of his bee-craft. He also repeated to me a wish latterly —a very bee-like wish—that he should "die in harness."

He became ill, and I watched his hives for him, for it was spring. I used to sit by his bed and report to him on the state of his hives, while he lay in a flannel night-shirt buttoned up to the neck, looking out of the window which showed only the sky from where he lay, gazing for the first time in his life, I think, on the passing pageant of clouds. "In bee-keeping," he said for the last time to me, though I believe he' thought it was the first, "there's one great rule to remember, 'Take time by the forelock.'"

I was making an artificial shower of rain with a syringe and a pail of water out of a cloudless sky, which caused an absconding swarm to settle, which I captured and made ready for his thirteenth hive, when he died. For, though he smiled when I returned, it was not at my news. I saw by the fixity of his eyes towards the window that the clouds had beckoned him away at last.

We planted a willow over his grave, for that is the first thing the bees come to in spring, and if they know anything (and who knows how little or how great their apprehension?) they may guess that thereunder lies a Bee Master and a Master Bee.

Thereafter I backslid. For the swarm I had taken for his thirteenth hive was gone when I came to hive them. "But there's no accounting for bees," I told myself, looking at the deserted beginnings of comb under the lid of the box. I spoke of it to the postman when I went for the afternoon post.

"Oh, but of course," he said, "why, of course—they'd be sure to go. You see, you never told them of his death. If anyone dies in the house and you don't tell the bees, they won't stay."

And yet I couldn't scorn this old fellow, with his dark certainties and his ridiculous tinklings after bees that were really in his own bonnet. The old moralists bid us go to the bees for an example, but to one who has seen a little of the modern world their whole polity seems designed by God as a warning against the very contingency to which civilisation is now come.

For if you "understand" bees as John Pready "understood " them, and ever pause to look at the sky above, you realise what a blind alley of communistic effort their race represents. They are but another of Nature's disillusions. Blindly they serve the modern honey-factory, one grain of love in a desert of labour is their lot—honey is taken from them and they make more and more, and then when winter comes accept syrup for food.

Our postman said little as a rule, and then only when questioned. "Isle of Wight disease? Never heard of it. My bees? No, I never lost none. John Pready's? Why, of course they died; he used to feed 'em on syrup and faked-up stuff all winter, and in they cold, wooden hives. It's unnatural—stand to reason they died. You can't do just as you like with bees. They be wonderful chancy things; you can't ever get to the bottom of they."

And that is why, from my modern bee-keeping, I often look over the hedge at the straw-templed nook in the postman's garden, as one full-fed with scientific formulæ may look back on Eden, when darkness was a presence and Adam stood in awe of an ordaining Hand. For our postman's bees are endowed with a spirit and a caprice; they are his neighbours, not his slaves. If any in the house dies he tells them of it; if they fly away he makes a tinkling noise to charm them home. His lore is so immemorial as to make "science" seem an unmannerly upstart cocking snooks at venerable men. Virgil was persuaded of it, and the ancient Greeks, who endued bees with the gift of oratory. Did not a swarm of bees alight on the mouth of the infant Plato? Did not Mahomet admit them to Paradise? And Porphyry says of fountains, "They are adapted to the nymphs, or those souls which the ancients called bees."

Like a wise man, our postman admits of understanding less as he grows older. Least of all would he admit to understanding bees. One continues, of course, with one's modern utility hives, but his straw skeps with their Gothic curve are like the temples of some picturesque old faith. And, oh, who nowadays wouldn't prefer to be—as he is—still on the side of the angels?

CHAPTER X

IT was high summer. Tall as a single cliff stood the green-burdened elms, jagged and cragged with black sun-shadows, before which the gliding dove was like an allegory of faith in perilous places, at the feet of which our garden pool looked as small as a dropped hand-mirror.

The gipsy fruit hung on the cherry tree and the thin leaves fingered them. But they were for the birds to pluck ; *our* cherries were on a tree of a size it was possible to net.

It was like some close rich tapestry before our windows in the early mornings, the thick-woven fantasy of slender leaves, edged with those that floated like weak hands and blessed the air ; the green sharply decorated with the brilliant baubles, and with the figures of stiff-standing bright-eyed birds.

The tits were very busy with their thoughtless love-burden of five gaping throats to feed, in the hole in the trunk where they had built their nest.

And now came the owls. They had nested in the garden-side elms, and their young made a curious sound all day, but especially towards evening, as of a person breathing heavily in sleep. At twilight, as we sat still before our house, they came down upon the grass, two big brown owls and three fledglings. Every evening at the same hour they would come, and there would be flying instruction from the elders. They often had the greatest difficulty in making the

young ones pay attention, though. One of the parents
would fly a little way, then alight and look back for
the others to follow. But all their backs were turned.
So she returned and did her flight again and again,
until they condescended to observe her, and one would
be moved to raise its wings and give a compunctious
hop. Whereupon the other two would hop. Then
all three would hop, and turn and stand looking in the
other direction again. This while the father-bird
(surely it was the father) stood magisterially on a log
observing the progress of the instruction. The mother
was indefatigable. "See, this is the way to do it. Like
this. Oh, you aren't paying attention. Do please
look. Now watch me. There. Now try. Oh, you can
do much better than that if you like. See, like this."

She alighted on the log near papa, who shook his
feathers and seemed to recollect himself. "Asleep,
my dear? Nonsense. I was watching attentively."
He hopped down and joined the three recalcitrants.
"Now, children, you really must pay attention to
your mother. You are getting of an age when you
can expect to be beak-fed no longer. You must
seriously begin to equip yourselves for going out into
the world and earning your own living."

The mother had now recovered her breath and
started fluttering before them again. They dutifully
fluttered after her, while father strutted pompously
back to his log.

Soon, however, the young ones were infected with
the flying craze, and all the parents did was to stand
while the three flew from bough to bough and tree
to tree about their heads. Then one day they were
gone, parents and all.

The cuckoo, too, that at first often made our cherry
tree a halting-place, had changed his note and gone
farther off. In May he used to wake us up sometimes,
singing in the orchard. But the dove, with her opiate

murmur, her lull of heart's ease in romantic sorrow—
she was with us all the day.

. Now it was that in earlier days we should have been
preparing for the harvest. But our little corn was
hardly more than made it a picturesque vestige. Our
hay was carried; harvest was more autumnal now—
it was a root harvest: potatoes, sugar-beet, carrots,
as well as swedes and mangolds. The farm was half
factory-site, half vegetable-garden.

Joe Boxted was the first of us to grow sugar-beet.
Benfield was very conservative and for a long time
put no trust in the confident promises of the factories'
agents as they canvassed for contracts. Joe in the end
said he would grow a couple of acres, largely because
he had on his farm a field of that diminutive size which
was jocosely referred to locally as "The Thousand
Acres," and he did not know what else to grow on it.
In the spring he had always to brave the bluff greeting
of, "Well, Joe, have you set the Thousand Acres yet?"
There were eternal variations of the extravaganza.
"There's one thing, Joe, you'll not need to trouble
rolling that bit o' land; put your two feet down on it
nd the job's done."

Joe set the sugar-beet; but the soil was deep and
rich, with the result that the roots grew down to a
great depth. The summer was dry; the ground was
very hard; Joe had no sugar-beet lifter, nor was there
room to work one. "I'm told they're quite easy to
pull up by hand," he said. He found they weren't.
All day and every day for weeks, it seemed, I would
see Joe purple in the face straining at one of his sugar-
beet roots, each one of which was as firmly wedged as
Excalibur in the rock.

. "These bloody beet go down a mile into the earth,"
he cried, when I spoke to him, and "I'll never grow
another one as long as I live." And he didn't. Long
after he would grow hot in the face at the mention of

the industry; and when recounting his experience to
a stranger he so vividly relived the past—oaths and all—
that the stranger began to wonder with some misgiving
whether Joe saw any likeness to a sugar-beet agent in
him to account for the menace of his features.

Now young creatures of all kinds saw the world
and tried their limbs. After the half-light and straw
smell of the buildings the calves were pushed out into
the ecstasy of open day. Not that they wanted to go
at first. They did not recognise, in the oblong of light
that stood where the door had been, anything that was
less of a barrier. Every adult creature knows when
the way is open or closed—but not these; they had no
sense of solidity or non-solidity, and so our attempts
to drive them out were fruitless. We had to take
each one separately and heave him bodily through
the aperture before he could realise that it was one.
Once out into the wired grass enclosure they stood
stiff-legged in a dazzle of astonishment. They had
never seen the outer world before; the cow-shed annexe
had been but a second womb. Breezes combed the
willows' silver-green hair, made the briars dance,
slanted over the rose-cups and spilled their dewy wine.
After the scuffling in the stuffy shed it was a blaze of
freedom.

A moment's trance, and then with concerted, strangled
bleats from their throats—not the plaintive call of
hunger, but a cry of ecstasy which seemed only just
sub-human in its attempt at articulation—they dashed
away cocking their tails high into the air.

Then was manifested the reason for the fencing of
resilient wire. They saw no obstacle in anything and
charged the fence in a body. It flung them back like
a catapult. Panic seized them and they fled in the
opposite direction, only to be similarly repulsed.
Gradually it dawned on them that there were inexplic-
able boundaries to their world. Rather it seemed

that there was an enemy, invisible but agile, who behaved against them as they behaved. They rushed, and he rushed at them; they walked, and he quite gently repulsed them. After a number of these setbacks—the perfect parable of young zeal and earthly destiny—they stood hardly daring to move, or, if they did, stepped forward with comic timidity, sniffing every inch of the air with outstretched necks and jerking back with apprehension.

But then they discovered that the green stuff they stood on was wonderfully good to eat, ·and left such advanced scientific problems as the density of matter for later investigation.

It was really surprising how quickly they did learn that when there was a square brightness they could go through it, when blackness, not; and that four threads of wire meant "no farther." For in a few days, though they would go scattering out into the paddock like wild autumn leaves, they would draw up promptly at the fence.

It is not only the verdant air of summer that begets such frenzies. A dozen or so adult cattle will sometimes be sent quite mad by the torment of flies. I witnessed such an occurrence when six bullocks which Harry Russet was fattening on the grass came crashing through my hedges one windless noon. They were lashing the air with their tails and bellowing, while they galloped at frantic speed, and one realised in a moment that here was something more awesome even than the Gadarene swine rushing into the sea. They neither deviated nor slackened, and trampled down everything in their path—would have me, too, as I tried to stop them, if I had not jumped aside in time. Close after them came Harry on his horse, spurring his hardest and not stopping for a look or a word. Yet he could not make up on them.

Later he returned, having brought the cattle to a

standstill, he told me, about eight miles away. His horse was exhausted, so was he. "As for them, you'd never know them for the same cattle. They went straight as a crow flies from here right the way to Ribland Marsh, and even then I don't reckon they'd have stopped if it hadn't been for the river. It was the flies done it. All at once I see them cock their tails, and away they went. They were worth twenty pound apiece when they left here, and now they aren't worth ten." Indeed, the creatures that were brought back next day were not recognisable for the fine beasts that had stood in Harry's meadow. They returned lank, loose-skinned, drooping, and ashamed: his fattening treatment had to start all over again. "They'll never properly get over it, though," he said.

How deserted the farmyard looks in summer, when all its inhabitants lie abroad in the fields by day and night. Its gates are flung wide, its lesser doors flap idly, and within there is only short, parched straw. Its life is but sparrows and the farm cats stalking them. What a contrast to the January scene, when behind the fast gates all the animals stood huddled from the snow. Even the pigs I had put out into the meadow, where the young ones trotted through the long grass and filled their days with alarms at scuttling rabbits or others of their kind met unexpectedly in the undergrowth. The sows sought the waterside and lay under the trees in beds of cool mud, their ears over their eyes, grunting in unclean satisfaction.

But first it was necessary to ring their snouts to prevent them rootling up the meadow. This is an ear-splitting task, for though their snouts are callous pigs always squeal as soon as handled, and their voices have a note which vibrates the human ear-drum to the point of physical pain. This noise often comes apt for rural simile. Walter, who like most other countrymen installed a wireless set, referred to the B.B.C. dance orchestra slightingly on the ground that "some of them instruments they play shriek worse than a pig in a gate."

"There's nothing, to my thinking," said Walter, "like a good loud brass band."

In fact, we felt quite deserted—for being a true farmhouse Silver Ley in each of its two living-rooms had a window looking out to the back at the yards, as well as one giving on to the front grass-patch with its roses. It was companionable, even patriarchal, to see the cattle and horses neighbouring us out there. As winter afternoons drew to twilight it would have seemed much more to us that we were living in solitude but for their occasional rustles, snorts, and stampings in the yard.

Some of our cattle we hardly saw all summer, for I had hired the paddocks of the empty manor of Benfield so that some of mine might be saved for hay. With the many present activities of our life it was quite easy to forget all about them, and one evening I said to Nora, "Do you know we haven't seen those cattle for two months? I find by the entry in my account-book that it is just eight weeks to-day since they were sent down there. Let's take a walk and see how they are getting on."

Nora agreed, and we walked over the fields to the park. The great gates of wrought iron—the work of a former Benfield smith—were locked, but I rang the bell and the lodge-keeper opened them for us. Or, rather, I pulled at the bell which made such a jangling in its rusty guides that the lodge-keeper heard, and we all pushed at the gate to open it far enough to let us through. I apologised for the fuss that we had caused by using this instead of the back entrance which he used; but it seemed an empty scruple to walk half round the park to enter that way, with the manor a blind shell and its front gates the first we came to.

The old lodge-keeper, though, was delighted, and bustled about to undo them as though a fine equipage and impatient horses fumed outside. Indeed, that was probably how the last lady he had admitted to the precincts of the mansion had arrived. Certainly the first, for he was really very old now—older than he looked, for his face was smooth with a life of quiet and encompassed duty, and it was not until one saw right into it that many years seemed added on to him. For he lived alone in his little lodge behind the luxuriant prison-grating of the gates, and his face had the calm pale stare of moonlight through long looking at un-answering things.

A narrow curving lake crooked the manor lawns in its cold arm, which we crossed by a grass-matted bridge and viewed our cattle in the park beyond. They had done well, and besides looked fine and genteel among the oaks. Then I thought—I don't know why—they'll be glad to be back at home, though of course it did not matter to them where they were if the grass was good and plenty. But then I realised that the windows of the tall square house overlooking the place oppressed me with their blankness. For curtained, inhabited windows do not stare at one so hungrily—they are like eyes that signal of the life within; but when there is none, but echoing emptiness only, their look is like that of death—or madness; like the eyes of our guide that had nothing but waiting in them.

"The lake," I said as we re-crossed the bridge, "keeps wonderfully clear of weed."

"The canal," he said, "is very deep."

"The lake," I said, "this lake."

"Yes, the canal," he answered.

"Why do you call it the canal?" I asked. "It's not a canal; it's a lake."

"It's always been called the canal," he said, and would have it so. I wondered how the name had arisen. It certainly looked like a chopped-off length of a canal. Yes, to one standing on the bridge, the name was really a *mot juste*. Yet there was no canal within fifty miles of the district, so I surmised it must be another example of that instinctive genius which possessed the semi-articulate, as Nature the earth; the same that children have, which can light up the true nature of a thing with a word that is like the flash of spring flowers in a winter glade.

The lodge-keeper went ahead of us now, and I called to him how well he kept the lawns.

"I do what I can," he said, and added, "It wouldn't take long to make the place look proudly again. It isn't as though it's a place that's gone to ruin. There wouldn't be any chance then. But it's still a place anybody might take a fancy to."

It was a curious medley of dishevelment and neatness. Lank roses made extravagant obeisance to us across the paths, yet the edging of the lawn that curved before the house was clean-cut.

"I'm glad you came by the gates," he said. "I must look to them. I didn't realise they'd got so stiff."

He was leading us away across the grass. "The stables," he said, "I should like you to see the stables." We followed him, though there was little enough to see: an empty corridor of loose-boxes which echoed loudly the scurrying of a rat.

"This is where I started," said the lodge-keeper. "I came as a stable-boy first. The master kept a dozen horses or more, and he'd always be round first thing of a morning to see they was all right. Yes, we had to be up betimes. That's where Day Star ruined herself." He stooped and showed us an old scar along the wood. "Someone left a fork in the box, and she stamped on it, and then she started a-kicking. I got the blame for that."

We bent and examined the mark and murmured

sympathetically. We found that through some suggestion of the gloom and emptiness and silence we were
talking in the undertones of people conversing in a
church.

"Well," I said loudly to break the spell, "we must
be getting back now."

At that moment a hollow yell sounded from the
lawn; we looked out in time to see a peacock floating
up into a walnut tree, whence his tail with its hundred
eyes hung down like a discarded fan.

Our guide smiled. "He's company to me."

He led us on through yew-walks as deep as smug-
glers' caves, then out suddenly into a bright space of
all innocent flowers—bachelors' buttons, marigolds,
pansies, crowding to look up at us. Then an avenue
of great languid roses detaining us at every step to
spill on us their stored quicksilver of yesterday's shower.
Past a little maze of quick hedge—an eighteenth-century
conceit, overgrowing into a fortress.

"You can get lost in there," said the lodge-keeper.

We had no doubt of it, we answered.

Everything was there, waiting—greenhouses, apple-
house, potting-sheds, the great vegetable garden with
its smiling red wall. Thence by polite degrees of bush
fruit, nuttery, shrubbery, we graduated back again to
the formality of a pool and a little statue all alone before
the terrace. The stone nymph making her gesture of
languor set the tone wherewith we mounted slowly
the well-preserved steps, at the top of which the bas-
relief Doric pillars of the manor awaited us with theatrical
hospitality. As we climbed, in my mind's eye I saw
the life, and what our guide and his vanished generation had desired—a captain. Still he lived laborious
days sweeping and garnishing—for who knoweth when
the master cometh?—a prophet in the wilderness trust-
ing still in the return of that earthly patrician Messiah
to set up his kingdom there.

Had circumstances been other, my Nora, I was saying to myself, what a golden duty you would have made of it. It was all the more startling to be met by the faces of two sheep on the top step, who scrambled to their feet and rushed past us with a clatter down the steps and off into the twilight.

"We must be getting back now," I said again; but the old lodge-keeper was already holding the tall house-door open for us. We went in, and he talked us through the house, until he had talked himself into the illusion that he was showing over possible, nay, every minute more probable, purchasers.

He praised furniture and friendliness into these blank dusk spaces, but his best effect he saved for upstairs.

"You've no need to worry about water-supply," he said, "and all such arrangements"; opening at the same moment with either hand the neighbouring doors of closet and bathroom. He turned on the taps; they gushed. "Excellent," we commended. "And see here," he said. He pulled the plug of the water-closet and turned to us with a triumphant smile as the house echoed with the demonstrably efficient deluge.

We came out again, and it was dark. We started towards the gates, the lodge-keeper following us, now fallen silent at last after the sweet illusion of Somebody-Come-to-See-Over-the-Place. He detained us yet once more, beside the nymph. "There was a wing of the house stood over there on that raised part," he said. "But that was pulled down—and I'll tell you for why." He told us the story of the son of the squire of the manor who had first employed him as a boy. For the son came of age, and thereafter the place which had been very quiet for many years was enlivened with the laughter of young men and women by day in the gardens; and by night the windows were brilliant, and there was music and song.

After the affair of Day Star, our guide had been

relegated to the gate-house; but he was not one to pine, and soon found life full of interest in the many comings and goings of those days, when the bell-pull was kept polished with the grasp of a continuous sequence of hands.

Of all to whom he opened there was none so gay, so beautiful, so gracious, as the daughter of Sir Giles Winthrop who lived in the town of Stambury. No party within the twelve-mile radius of a carriage-journey was considered complete without Mary Winthrop —certainly none at Benfield Manor. The memory of her kindled again the lodge-keeper's eyes from the light stare into which they had relapsed after the tour of the house.

"She'd always have a word for you as she went by," he said; "she'd talk to you just as though you were her equal. She weren't a mite proud."

She was as admired as her father was respected in the life of the market town. Theirs had been one of those high Georgian houses past which Nora and I strolled when there was half an hour to waste after the business of the market. We identified it; borough offices now in part, and part a flat, and the top-storey windows blank and dusty.

"Ah, the parties there used to be at Benfield Manor in those days," mused the lodge-keeper. "Skating parties in the winter when the canal were froze, with coloured lanterns all round it and a basket of red coals at the side. Then the moon came up and they'd be there till near midnight. 'Twas as pretty a sight as ever I did see."

In the end Mary Winthrop accepted the squire's son, Richard Firbank, in marriage. The wedding took place in the Abbey church of Stambury, and it was on a scale that made it the event of the year.

"Well, the old squire, he died not long after, and Mr. Richard and his wife come to live at Benfield Manor."

131

"But why did he pull the wing down?" I asked, for it was getting late.

"Ah, he didn't pull it down," said the lodge-keeper, and became sunk in reminiscence and half-forgetful of us.

"There weren't any vice in him, really. I'll stand for that—'twere just that he were weak—weak as water."

We gathered that Mary Firbank, like others, had been beautiful and gay in youth only as in compensation for coming sorrow. The roystering companions who had added to the gaiety of those early parties became, one or two of them, a danger. Gay bachelordom towards middle-age becomes known by less salubrious terms. A married man to be happy must live in a different stratum. These few, the years bringing no compensations for grey hairs, grew hilarious to desperation. They would not leave Richard and Richard was too weak to leave them.

A lodge-keeper sees a good deal of life and learns to judge of the company that stands at the gates. There was the lady, too, who strolled alone in the grounds, or with her child in hand; who sat on the terrace waiting, or near the French windows that looked towards the gates. She grew no less gracious, but her smile came more slowly and more wan.

Other little things a servant sees; field-gates that used to be kept painted growing shabby, buildings in disrepair; then larger things—horses sold, a groom and a gardener dismissed. Then a whole herd of cattle sold.

Our lodge-keeper now was married: his wife was one of the maids at the manor, and she reported to him a sentence or two she had heard by chance as she went about her business. Through a half-open door the words in her mistress's voice, "Never mind, there is my chest of silver—that should be worth . . ." Her master interrupted in quick expostulation, "Not for a moment—never on any account."

There was a great iron box locked away in a far attic full of heirlooms of the Winthrop family, of whom Mary had been the only child—so it had been discovered later belowstairs; up to this time it had been just a large heavy box among other boxes; up to the time, that is, when Mrs. Firbank took the lodge-keeper's wife into the room where it was kept to help her get to it. They moved a box or two from before it. "Now just help me shift it an inch or two from the wall so that it will open—it's very heavy." They stooped to it, and it rose in their hands an empty shell.

"The silver had been stolen?" I said.

He shook his head. "Mr. Richard had been selling it, bit by bit, for years."

"That were the night of the county ball at Stambury, when my missis told me about that there box. You see it weren't broken into nor nothing, so the mistress seemed to know just how things were. She never said nothing to my missis, only 'Thank you, Jane; you can go now.' But I see her as they drove out in the carriage all dressed for Stambury, and she did look strangely, I thought. She always were made much of at Stambury, and the coachman told me how when they got there what a crowd there was all round the door; but when she was seen to step out of the carriage somebody cried out, 'Make way for Mrs. Firbank,' and they made way as it might have been for the queen herself."

That same night she fell, by chance or not, out of her bedroom window. "I found her, sir, next morning, lying just where we are standing now.

"Oh, dear, that were a terrible time. Mr. Richard, he were like a crazed thing for days. Then he left all of a sudden. He never came back no more. Everything had to be sold.

"Then Squire Lindley came. His daughter used to sleep in that wing, and she'd wake screaming in the night, crying that she'd seen two hands coming out of the wall at her by the window. Other people said they heard groaning and such-like—well, you know how a story like that gets about. The servants got so that they wouldn't go into the wing after dark, and in the end Squire Lindley had it pulled down to put an end to it all.

"But, Lord, there weren't no harm in the place." The old lodge-keeper drew a flute from his pocket and put it to his lips. He played, then looked up, pleased with himself. "You wonder how I come to know that, sir? That was what Mrs. Firbank used to sing when she come about here as a girl. You must know, sir, there weren't no organ in Benfield church in those days, and we chaps used to make all the music there was; that's how I come to learn the old flute." He played the tune over again, sitting on the stone rim of the pool whence the nymph rose as though conjured by his ditty. I just recognised "The Lass with the Delicate Air." He looked up, pleased, after he had faltered through it again. "Ah, but you should have heard her sing it. It went frolicsome the way she sung it. Bless you, sir, there weren't no harm in the place." He shook out the flute, and put it to his lips again, his old eyes wrinkling in charmed reminiscence. We bade him good-bye and set off home. For some way we still heard his owlish wood-notes haunting the night.

CHAPTER XI

A LITTLE way back I likened a ploughed fallow to a
choppy sea. It is more so than ever in the summer, if
not to the onlooker, to him who cultivates it. For one
does not keep the earth bare by not sowing it, but only
by continually moving it with the harrows. Now the
earliest form of harrow was a ponderous thing of teeth
set in a wooden frame, very different from the modern
small frames of snaky iron chained together with teeth
scientifically graduated. But the old wooden frame
persists in one instance, that is in the thing called an
A-harrow. Its shape is triangular—three beams iron-
clamped. Its teeth are about a foot long and an inch
thick. Actually its extent is comparatively small,
and anybody observing it in operation might wonder
that four of the best horses are needed to pull it. It
provides one of the stiffest jobs on a heavy-land farm,
and, though the man in charge has only to sit and drive,
it is by no means what might be called a "cushy" job
for him, despite a chaff-bag well stuffed with straw
for seat.

I remember in my childhood a side-show at the old
White City Exhibition called "Witching Waves."
Here for the sum of sixpence you were put aboard a
small wheeled craft and left to cope as best you could
with the continuous upheavals of the floor. As a
farmer I have wondered at the number of sixpences I
spent on this (sixpences were pounds to the child)
which Nature now provided for nothing. The baked

fallow rocked me to and fro on my triangular craft like an ancient Briton in his coracle. It would ride up and balance on some monster clod, then over and down lop-sided into a depression. Sometimes a particularly tenacious one would catch between the back teeth and wring it sideways, so that, perched on one's chaff-bag, one had to hold one's body balanced as ready as a sailor's in a storm.

The teeth turned up blanched and agonised roots that had been living secretly in moist places, exposing that moisture, too, to the torrid air.

After a day of this our horses were glad of Sunday's rest, as were the two I had borrowed from Bob Chilgrove to make up my team. Our Kitty looked no bigger than a foal standing in the meadow beside them, yet not only did they not despise her, but often she was the leader. For she had regained a well-being which manifested itself in moments of caprice, and made her more companionable than when she had been just a spiritless drudge. Suddenly it would be as if the air had spoken to her, and she'd lift her front feet from the ground, shake her mane, and away in a stumpy little gallop. The other two, feeding with bent necks, would fling up their heads with the resilience of a short bow, and chase after her as though the devil were at their heels, ending up tamely enough at the brink of the pond, and looking in upon themselves.

In the hot weather they would stand alongside one another, face to tail, to keep away the flies. They performed that office for Kitty too. Her tail had been unkindly docked. Even if it hadn't, it would only have kept the flies from Captain's knees. All the same, she flicked it industriously to and fro, and seemed satisfied that the others were deriving great benefit.

For some reason the horses considered the ducks fair game when they issued from under the hedge into the meadow in querulous procession, their bodies inclined grotesquely forward at the angle of some pieces of agricultural machinery. Suddenly they would be spotted by the three, whose scamper received thereby an immediate purpose. Before the white ducks had time more than to call a halt and take a survey the hooves would be upon them, and they would scatter like a burst of spray.

After one or two wings had been broken I had to wire them out of the meadow. Wire netting solves so many small problems of the farmyard that I often wonder what the farmer did before it was invented. Yet he had the reputation of being, on the whole, a smiling, cheery fellow. It should have been the rats and the rabbits who smiled.

Not the least of my farming problems was the chronic one of the Cats and the Kind-hearted Mistress. "A good cat is worth five pounds on a farm," is an adage of agriculture. Each of the major buildings has its own cat, which thereby becomes known by the name of its haunt. Thus there was the one at Silver Ley who lived in the cow-house. She was known in the terms of Suffolk abbreviation as the "cow-'us" cat. She was old—she died, but left a daughter to inherit her home and duty. She, then, was known as the "cow-'us kit." From this she became known for short as just "Cow'us."

There was one that crouched, a blacker shadow, in the barn; a sandy, lionish one that burned at you from a beam of the granary; a stable cat. All were wild and fierce and fearful, starting like leaves at a strange tread. All except the "cow-'us kit." Her mother had been tabby-coloured, but with a Persian wealth of fur. The kitten, however, was just sleek and gentle tabby, with rather a foolish, trustful face, and a tail that stood up straight as a staff and curled itself into a little hook at the tip. There never was anything less

predatory than "cow-'us." She would stand on the
wall and wait to rub herself against anyone who passed;
and that was about all she did. This may have been
the enervating result of the daily ration of warm new
milk in an old tin that Walter gave her, for which she
would sit and wait beside him, listening to the chime
of the milk jets spurting into the pail from the cow's
udder. Either that—for this had been a largesse her
mother had enjoyed without moral deterioration—or
she was the daughter of some village woman's fireside
tom.

For awhile all our three cows were dry, and the
"cow-'us" kitten's coat began to stare and she looked
gaunt. She made no attempt, apparently, to shift for
herself, and, when Nora remarked on her poor
appearance, I growled like any hard-hearted Hodge
that the remedy was in her own claws. But Nora
took her her ration of milk from our house supply
which we bought temporarily from neighbour Russet.
"Cow'us" soon traced the supply to its new source,
and would be found sitting at the back door as though
to save Nora the trouble of going to the cow-house.
Unfortunately the granary cat observed "Cow'us"
feeding at the house door, and crept by cautious degrees
nearer, and found that there were good things to be had
there. As I opened the door there would be a yellow
flash, and I would see two amber eyes watching me
from the black interior of an outhouse. As soon as
my back was turned she would be ousting "Cow'us"
from the milk again. Gradually she grew less afraid.
The barn cat somehow heard of this, and then the
stable cat, and soon, whenever one opened the door,
there would be a multi-coloured burst of flight, leaving
"Cow'us" blandly gazing up at one beside a depleted
saucer. But, as I say, the cats grew less and less afraid,
until they all sat in a semi-circle round the back door.
Nor would they flee as one went out; on the contrary,

they would rise up, give a mew in unison, and close in
about one's feet. One's progress was clogged by their
importuning bodies. In the buildings rats and mice
increased and rioted. The stacks were all a-scuffle. I
protested against this feeding, but Nora pointed out
that "Cow'us" would starve else.

"Feed her indoors," I suggested—unfortunately
though, for it now became a game of Tom Tiddler's
Ground. As soon as the door was opened to admit
"Cow'us," the whole group would streak in, seize
whatever they could, and hide away under oven, cupboards, chairs, in preparation for a similar dash out
again.

The end was not yet. The majority of these cats
were, as cats usually seem to be, of female sex, and
gave birth. As soon as their kittens were able to walk
they led them down from their birthplaces among the
straw and chaff to the back door of the house, pointing
that out to them as the source of all good things, rather
than instructing them to rely upon their teeth and claws
for sustenance. Soon we had, not five mild and bene-
volent creatures squatting at the door, but twenty.
And still they came. We were besieged. Drown them
as soon as they were born? Yes—but first to find them;
for their mothers acquired an artfulness in hiding them
in the beginning equal to that in leading them to the
house later. There is a stage in a kitten's growth when
one can no longer drown it without a revulsion—that
time when it looks at you with wide china-blue eyes.
It was not till then that the mothers led them to us in
procession, mewing on encouragingly the fainthearted.

Later it became apparent that those who were not
long ago kittens were themselves about to be fruitful.
Something had to be done—either drowning *en masse*
or shooting, both equally distasteful. I took out my
gun. The cow-house kitten was the first to present
herself, blinking and smiling in the sun with the large

content of impending maternity. I aimed, and she observed me placidly along the barrel. I could not. I tried the sandy old cat who used to lurk so wildly in the granary. She approached and rubbed herself against my legs. I have shot rabbits by the score, and hares even that mew most piteously when wounded, but I cannot shoot a cat. I put up my gun and put off the problem yet another day.

But luck awaited me. There drove up a boisterous young man whom I recognised as Major Russet's nephew. He had lately started as a farmer—taking over one of the dilapidated farms of the district at a nominal rental, and was full of assurance of making things "go" by ingenious cutting of costs. It was indeed a time for the young and opinionated, for their elders could no longer point to the proven success of traditional procedure. In fact the tables were turned, and in their despair they listened to the young men who brought technicalities of agricultural mass production from their colleges, as to prophets, inspected their hundred-yard-long "battery brooders" where chickens lived on wire trays from a few days old to killing time without ever seeing the outer world.

Young Gerald came straight to the point. "Will you sell me a sack of cats?" he called out as I went to meet him.

"Sell!" I cried. "I will give you two sacks." Had I been a farmer from birth I should not even in this have so far forgotten myself as to miss the chance of a deal.

"I'm eaten up alive with rats at Challey Moat," he said, "and uncle advised me to come to you if I wanted any cats—said he'd seen a few round your house-door!"

I called to Walter to bring a sack, and he held the mouth open while we popped them in—black, black and white, white, ginger, ginger and white, and every shade of tabby.

"There, a coomb of cats," laughed Gerald as he tied the sack.

"Better weigh them, master," Walter added. "I reckon he's got overweight."

He drove away with his animated bundle, like the man going to St. Ives, and I turned back with a sigh of relief to the depopulated doorway. The sun shone only on one half-empty enamel dish. But when I looked again the solitary cow-house kitten had appeared as from nowhere and was lapping at it in a reverential attitude. She owled up at me, licking her whiskers.

"We thought you a fool," I said to her, "but the serpent couldn't have been subtler to attain its end. No more of this disastrous ambiguity 'Cow'us'—henceforth you are the house cat." I opened the door and she trotted in, as contented cats do trot, her forepaws doing a very quick goose-step and her tail carried, as I have mentioned, erect like a staff with the tip forming a little hook, the meaning of which, in the language of tails, I have never been able precisely to discover.

We had such deluges in August as divided the gravel paths into stream-beds. The wet made the hens as unhappy as the winds of March had done, when they used to crouch under the lee of things and make as difficult a crossing of any open stretch as a full-rigged ship unable to furl a sail. We thanked God we had but little corn to carry. Things looked very lean that month. On an arable farm, whatever the market price of corn, the expanse of swaying ears that surge round the house as far as the eye can see looks like a flood of plenty. But, on an arable farm converted, black hen-houses on fields of thin new grass give it rather that blighted air of country on the edge of an industrial town. Added to that, wet weather making the hens look sad as ruined ladies' hats, and laying what corn there is flat to the ground. It rained for four days and nights without ceasing, and after that Joe Boxted, Bob Chilgrove, and I met where our three holdings joined, looking like three seamen in our oil-skins and rubber boots. We were all out to see the extent of the damage and sardonically outvied one another. "Your oats? Ah, but just look at that bit of barley of mine," Joe cried. Bob said, "My Revetts wheat is as flat as your hand."

So we had a strenuous and old-fashioned harvest after all, for six acres Walter and I and a hired man had to cut with the scythe, days of real heart-purging toil. I would half-wake in the night and feel myself still swaying with the motion of it, and hear, as I sunk back into dream, the rip and ring of the scythe-blade shearing through the coarse stalks.

We had only one scythe proper; but "you don't need to buy a new one," said the old man who came to work for me that harvest. He came walking with a sinuous staff as tall as himself. "I thought," he said, "as I worked in the woods last winter as how this'd make a good snathe for a scythe, whoever lived to want one; so here it be, master." He remembered, also, when last he was at the blacksmith's, seeing an old scythe-blade hanging among the medley of iron that decorated his walls. Such old men as he have an observation and a memory which stores up the where-abouts of innumerable "bits of things" that might one day come in useful. The formula for such a mental recording is ". . . and I thought to myself as I passed, 'That might come in handy one day.'"

So I gave Tom a little for the snathe twisted by Nature for the hand of man; and I gave the blacksmith a little for the blade and the setting of it properly on the handle. I felt hardly more than one generation from Adam, using that rugged arm of a tree as we stooped over the rain-beaten corn, advancing haltingly a stubborn step at a time, as though one's feet were pulled forward resistingly by the main force of the arm's swing.

Tom went behind us and gathered up the corn into sheaves, taking a few straws from each to tie it with. So we worked in the steamy sunlight on the soaked ground for a week or more. Then we carted the corn in many loads, for the sheaves were long, and, as Tom said, "homely" (in the sense of ugly, irregular, "made at home"), and the wagon went heavily; the wheels gathered up the earth like dough, wattled with stubble.

As we put the last sheaf on the stack, I handing it up from the wagon to Tom, who handed it to Walter, the men exclaimed as they exclaimed every harvest, "So that's the one we've been looking for all this time." Walter added, as he surveyed the finished stack from the ground, "There's been as much sweatin' for that little as when the whole farm was of corn."

I paid Tom off, who then betook himself to the outhouse of his cottage till another job turned up, or work in the woods began again, whittling away at walking-sticks there in the meantime. Always as he worked in the woods he had an eye for a likely bit of ash or thorn, and the rafters of his shed were hung with hundreds of them seasoning and awaiting his days of idleness. Then he would polish their bark, and for some make knobs decorated with poker-work designs, while the ends of others he would hold over scalding steam and bend into crooks. Sometimes Nature herself would offer a freakish suggestion. Here, say, was a thorn that grew complete with a queer knobby handle. By deft carving he would accentuate the knobbiness into a comic, snoutish face.

He walked great distances, taking a bundle of sticks into a wayside inn when the men were gathered for the evening, laying three on the table. Each man would stake twopence, and the matter would be decided on the quoit board, the winner taking his choice of the sticks, and the next two in their order. Tom would pocket the stakes, take up his sticks and stir his stumps to the next inn along the road.

The farmers would often hail him with, "Got a new stick for me, Tom?" Many a hall-stand in the vicinity was a museum-case of his quaint craftsmanship.

I have one which I prize, I have grown so familiar with it. It has been so many miles with me; a rough thing, all notches. Tom did not think it a good effort of his—"very homely"—but to me it has a satisfying look. When we were working at the laid corn Nora used to bring us tea at five o'clock, and on the last day of harvest Tom produced a stick which he presented to her. Now, his homely sticks were, as I say, admirable, but Nora being a "lady," and the occasion being a special one, he had been to great pains to make the gift, as he thought, suitable. He had chosen a slender stick, smoothed it, and coated it with sticky-looking red varnish—more, he had cut a strip of tin, and nailed it round in imitation of the silver band that decorates the shopman's article. The effect was deplorable, but of course Nora had to be extravagant in her admiration and thanks, for obviously he thought it the finest stick he had ever made.

But this scorn of the "homely" is usually confined to the young of the village. Mrs. Chilgrove's maid had a young man, a mechanic who lived in Stambury. This young man was to be entertained to tea at her home in the village, and Mrs. Chilgrove offered to let her make a cake for the occasion in her kitchen with its modern stove. The maid thanked her, but politely demurred. The reason was that it was not village etiquette to offer home-made cakes to one you desired to impress—that was a sign of "poorness." No, you turned out a tin of salmon and maybe a tin of sardines, procured iced cakelets of various hues from the town shop, and received your visitor with the consciousness that you were doing things in the grand, up-to-date manner, albeit that your roof was thatch and your lintel low.

There is, luckily, the weight of the Women's Institute movement to counter this "modernity" neurosis.

It was one of those mischances which cannot always be avoided, that all our three cows were dry just at this time. Seeing that we didn't afford a back-house boy our milk came to us from Harry Russet's farm down the road in various ways. Sometimes Walter would bring it; but it was not always ready in time; sometimes one of Harry's men would be passing; if neither the one nor the other, then Nora would go for it herself. In the lull after getting the corn, and before the root harvest, I would sometimes accompany her.

It was a season of such sudden gusty showers coming trailing on the wind that often we would be marooned under a tree half-way. But, as usual, memory prefers to count only the sunny hours, and I recall that half-mile there and back as a pleasant pilgrimage—a holiday between strenuous times, with plenty of small happenings in the lane which ordinarily one was too pre-occupied to notice, and a disposition in ourselves to "stand and stare."

In days of prosperity farmers used to take a week off at the seaside between hay-harvest and corn-harvest; in times of leanness I found there was no less interest in taking one at home.

The kitten always would follow, leaping about and arching its back at everything, being suddenly transformed, as cats are out-of-doors, from a purring domestic pet into a wild, startled creature, as spasmodic as a leaf in a gust.

The rook which I had shot in the spring and suspended from a stick to stop others stealing the hen's eggs, was growing daily more dilapidated and less like a

bird. For scarecrow time was now long past, that
windy time of old flapping clothes—for some reason
they always seem to be the remains of black formal
garments, frock coats, top-hats—in every approxima-
tion to the human form from a thing like a ghost to
a complete straw man, but always, somehow, gesturing
helplessness. The one in Harry's garden only yesterday,
it seemed, stood brandishing a mock gun, a phantom
threat of slaughter. Now it had dropped its gun,
and sagged comfortably among the tall peas and
beans as one sleeping the sleep of intoxication. Such
signs put one in mind of how quickly the summer had
flown.

The kitten only comes as far as the garden gate,
knowing that there are dogs within. She takes possession
of a stone-heap as usual, and having climbed to the
top sits licking her paws while she waits. Harry's
oak stick leaning against the wall of the house, and his
two dogs beside it, are sure signs that he is inside.
The dogs have long ceased to bark at us as at strangers;
they just put out their tongues and grin. But the small
fowls of all kinds that hang about the yard never will
realise that we are not the person who feeds them.
They come running as fast as they can, so that one
arrives at the back door at the head of a procession.
Their elders though, being wiser, have already hopped
over into the pig-sties where the pigs are sleeping their
breakfast off, wedged tightly together in the sun. There
they peck daintily at the small insects that crawl upon
their hides without waking any of the sleepers.

Knuckle-dusters would be of great use in the country
—not that one is likely to be set upon in these leafy
lanes, but the farmhouse door seldom has a knocker,
and it is sometimes quite painful to make oneself heard.
The door belongs to that kind of kitchen-breakfast-
room which is the busiest room in a farmhouse, and
when it opens reveals a brick floor, a cooking-range,

mahogany arm-chairs, a window overlooking the orchard and the beehives (very useful in swarming time)—a clear green window, with all the light coming in through heaving masses of leaves—and another window looking out on the yard, at the thatch of the barn and its great sagging doors. Here is the family—Harry at a late breakfast; his wife doing up butter in pounds; two youngsters putting on their satchels for school; and Jenny, the eldest, who runs across to the dairy to fill our jug.

She told us that the separator went wrong suddenly the night before, and the milk came spurting all over the dairy bricks; so now they had to employ the old method of skimming it till the separator was put right. The milk lay in wide shallow pans under the window, calm as ivory. The churn stood there too, with crumbs of butter sticking to it inside. For butter when it first forms is all in little crumbs which are patted into a solid mass afterwards. It looked very beautiful in there—the pure milk, the boxes of eggs in eternal variety of shades from white to brown. There is no calm, I think, like the calm of a cool dairy on a summer day. But Jenny thought not so. "Milk!" she cried. "I never drink milk; I hate the sight of it." But then Jenny had to live with it, and with the smell of it, to scald out the churn, and wash the spilt milk off the floor.

Jenny was hardly twenty. It seemed only the other day she was at school, and now she appeared to be almost the most important person on the farm. Her work was multifarious—the poultry, the dairy, the garden. She helped her mother in the house and her father in the fields. She interrupted washing-up the breakfast things to get our milk, and interrupted it again to run out and throw some water on two turkeys that had started to fight by the back door. Her life seemed all interruptions. In fact, the summer was a

memory of her flitting flaxen-haired through the rain
between house and buildings.

"Dazzling health" is a much overworked phrase,
but Jenny had it to an extent that made one forget
that hers is called the weaker sex. She had a strong
arm—but charm also, despite the fact that she had no
time to sit and cultivate it. Nature was her only beauty
specialist and hard work her school of deportment.
Yet the same which may age her before other women,
in the flood-tide of youth was an added flourish and
vital flush of beauty. In all but the length of her skirt
she was the same whom the man in the nursery rhyme
asked, "Where are you going to, my pretty maid?"
But now the reply was not, "'I'm going a-milking,
sir,' she said," but "I'm going hoeing sugar-beet."
Sugar-beet is an unromantic substitute for milking
under a tree; it is undoubtedly the ugliest crop that
has ever been grown in English fields. The only beauty
about it is the glow of the factory at midnight, working
full pressure extracting the sugar, while all the countryside sleeps.

But Jenny was never in such a hurry but she would
pull down some sprays of rambler roses hanging over
her garden wall, and stop at our cottage and hand them
in to us on her way to the fields, for our garden was
young as yet, and every blossom prized. She made
quite a picture sailing down the lane on her bicycle,
with her blue frock and flushed cheeks and the roses
in the hand that didn't hold the handle-bars. Her
hands were scratched, for she was not one who had
time to finick about snipping at blooms with a pair
of scissors. It just occurred to her as she went that
we might like them, and she pulled them down there
and then, giving pricks and scratches each a peremptory
suck, and on again down the lane.

"Isn't it time you took a day off?" Nora asked,
seeing her always at it.

"Well, you see, Father's got an extra five acres of sugar-beet this year," she replied, "and we all have to do our bit, hoeing them."

As she was the eldest she had the largest share. And the reason why her father set more acres of this laborious stuff was that the year before it was the only thing he grew that paid. The danger, though, was always that the profit might be outweighed by the labour on it causing other things to be neglected. Thus the convenience of having a reserve battalion of labour in the form of a family to press into service in emergency, when the weather was uncertain and things could only be done in snatches.

But, though Jenny was a farmer's daughter, she was by no means an uncouth wench. She did not even speak dialect. She was educated at the secondary school in the town near by. And then, curiously enough, as soon as she had grown up strong and capable, and had left school, she was swept into the vortex of the labour of the farm. And in these days when good farming and a brimming cornucopia were termed "over-production," it was a struggle to make two hundred acres pay, however many willing hands were at work on them.

Besides her domestic knowledge Jenny knew how to harness a horse for plough or shafts, and when fine days were rare and work pressing she was to be seen driving a pair on the roller, clad as ever in her trim bright frock. Farming is a kind of family Communism —she got no money for work which was quite as technical, really, as that of her cousin in London who worked in an office.

Yet I felt, somehow, that Jenny's secondary school education was not wasted, though she seemed to have turned her back on it. It had left her with an undaunted interest in life, which prevented the daily round hemming her in as with high walls. Her love of pretty

149

things and by-the-way things seemed to keep her still upon the crest of life.

One day on the crowded kitchen table I saw a pastel sketch of flowers, full of life and speed, like everything she did. I admired, and she told me she did it in odd moments. I was glad of the evidence that there were any. And on another day it happened that I arrived too early for the afternoon milk, so I sat and waited in the dining-room which was dim with beams, while the separator hummed outside, and Jenny showed me her sketch-book. There were flowers in it such as she would tear down from the generous bushes of her garden, loosening on herself showers from the late rain till she was like a picture of April, smiling through the drops on her face. But her sketch-book was her world too —there were scenes she had copied from books— mountains, lakes, eastern cities, and sands. She had coloured them to her own idea of how they must really look. Grey photographs in an encyclopædia had given her the clue to what lay beyond the lane and the little town where she went to school—the rest was her dream. This one, she said, she did after getting her father off at five-thirty a.m. on his day's holiday of the year—to the races; just as though the idea of travel had been infectious. She was always getting somebody off— her young brothers to school; her sister to dance at the fête; her father even. It seemed that all became equally helpless and childlike in her eyes when it came to getting dressed up and away for an occasion. I only hoped she would remember to get herself off on her wedding-day.

As to that, I was sitting with old Tom the woodman in the inn once when Jenny went by, and he remarked with a jerk of his thumb, "The chap wot marries her'll have to mind what he's arter."

"Why?" I asked.

"Well," he replied after another drink, "I reckon

she'd be able to give anybody a tidy lump o' the head if she had a mind to."

But Tom was old, and the allure and adventure of marriage nothing to him any more. Nor had he seen her sketch-book, with its perfect dawn and its perfect sunset. I hope she finds them both.

Temporarily Jenny had the benefit of the customers of our dairy—if benefit it could be called. The real trade in milk-retailing was done by Harry's brother Reuben, who had the milk-round of the district—a piece of enterprise on his part of which I shall speak later. But there were one or two cottagers (with many children) who sent for separated milk, which was very cheap, to help eke out their meagre budgets. For the nominal price of a penny they received their jugs full. Their shy and all but voiceless infants came for the milk, and on one occasion Nora put an orange into the hand of each of two cherubic young creatures, and the next day a bun from a tray just taken out of the oven. The day after, a small procession appeared at the end of the lane: every child of that cottage—they were seven—came for the milk.

"Careful, Nora," I said at the risk of appearing hard-hearted, "or it'll be worse than the cats."

I arrived at Jenny's dairy door one day just as she was tipping milk into these infants' jug in a great hurry. She handed it to them but no penny was forthcoming. They gazed up at her blankly for a minute, and at last one found strength to whisper, "The penny's at the bottom of the jug."

"Yes," I told her, "we've suffered from that." Their shyness was such that they would stand and say not a word while the milk was being poured on to the penny.

The way news travels in the country is almost telepathic. The mother of these children sent word to know if we could let her have a duck, as her sister who worked in town was coming to stay with her for a week of convalescence after an illness. Seeing that she was very poor, we charged her hardly cost price for the duck.

The day after, Jerry Hogbin the higgler drew up at our gate, and said he'd heard we had some ducks to sell!

Jerry had an old lanky mare this time, and what had once been a wagonette. He tried to sell me the mare. I think he thought that the more spavined the animal, the more likely I was to buy it out of sheer kindness. "Maybe we shall get a dry summer next year," he said, "and she'd do to horse your corn in."

"Horsing-in" the corn was a custom that seemed to have almost died out, either through the continuous wet seasons of late years, or, more likely, because no corn was cut loose nowadays. I remember it though, in Mr. Colville's great barn when I was a farm pupil. The summer was scorching and there was no fear of the corn heating, so we had one of the horses up on the stack with us as we packed it into the deep bays of the barn. All the while we worked there the horse walked to and fro and round and round on the corn, stamping it down. Thus it was possible to get nearly twice as much into the space than would have been the case otherwise, and that saved thatching. I remember feeling considerable misgivings, hearing him plunging about just behind me, and I on the edge of a stack of increasing height; but the horse was one as used to the job as his fellow who walked round and round in a circle all day working the elevator below, and he never lurched into us or got in our way.

I remember, too, some very dry loose barley—for even in my experience there were some of the older farmers who would never dream of tying barley into sheaves—I remember a great dapple-grey horse plunging among the froth of white straw, in which he sank almost to the shoulders; as he struggled out of it with difficult footholds, more kept piling up around him. All day his gigantic body wrestled with the flimsy straw.

All day as he worked the men would talk to him as well as to one another, encouraging him on; and by the time the stack was built one felt a fellowship for him above all the other horses of the farm. A steeply sloping gradient would be left in the side of the stack, and when the maximum height had been reached the stack-builder would urge the horse to the edge, and we'd give him a push, crying, "Down you go, Boxer," and he'd straighten his forefeet before him and sit on his haunches, and down he'd slide like a picture of an animal tobogganing in a child's book.

He would give a grunt when he got to the bottom, stand up and shake himself, and trot away to the pond to wash the dust from his throat.

CHAPTER XII

WE were making the best of a "tempest," as Walter called a rainstorm, in greasing the tumbril wheels under shelter of the cart-shed, levering each up with the great wooden jack, drawing the wheel off the iron arm of the axle-tree from which it slid with such ease, once unpinned, that I forgot its real weight and had to rally my strength sharply as it tilted over on to my arms, its wooden hub the size of a small cask, and its thick iron tyre. I held it so while Walter smeared the yellow grease on the axle, and as I waited my mind's eye saw again old Mark Ashen helping his men burn the tyre on to this wheel, for all his eighty years. He was the wheelwright in our little town, and had built this cart for me. Surely he was one of the last of his kind, I thought, seeing again the snowy side-whiskers through the smoke of the hot tyre on the wooden wheel, the strong wide intent face, the hammer lifted and clanging down on the tyre, hammering it over the wheel which lay raised on its side. At every stroke the men who held the hot tyre with irons moved the wheel round a few inches. Then the steam hissed up as water was poured over the tyre, cooling and contracting it to hold the wooden fellies fast together, and the old man laid his hammer aside unwearied.

Across the rafters of his sheds lay a great weight of seasoning timber, and beneath them segments of tree-trunks from which the hubs of wagon-wheels were carved out whole. His tumbrils were famous both for lightness of draught and long wear, but his trade in them had declined much of late owing to the under-cutting of larger firms. As Bob Chilgrove said to me, "He's a good workman but he's damn dear." And Mark Ashen said as we discussed the tumbril, "It's easy enough to make a cheap one of unseasoned wood and not trouble about the balancing of it, but I like to make one that's going to last. You know what cart paths are like in the winter on the heavy land; just think of the strain on a tumbril, loaded, and up to the axle-tree in mud. And then summer, and the ground like iron, and the sun scorching down on the wheels all day. Think, sir, if I was to make that sort of cart knocked up anyhow, and had to stand here at my gate and see my tumbrils going backwards and forrards, all to bits before the paint had hardly had time to wear off the bucks. No, I couldn't do that."

So he continued to make, when any resisted the lure of the cheap and momentary and ordered of him, things strong and to last. I went into his wood-store with him to select the timber for my tumbril. He smoothed his hand along one plank and another, murmuring, "Now that's a lovely piece of wood—that came out of Creevely Park in Lord Wenford's time." And he talked with his hand resting flat upon it as though it were a source of strength. He rolled the great tree-sections about like the segments of a shattered pillar, choosing two that should do for the hubs. We chose the axle-tree and the shafts. I think he felt that he would not have the opportunity of using much more of his plentiful store which father laid up for son (he was still using that which his father had stored), and liked to pick the very best to send out into this world of temporary values.

Indeed, the tumbril was a fine thing to own. I came into his yard when it stood finished, all pale clean naked wood. It seemed a pity that it could not be for ever like that; but next day it was red and green, and a few days later Mark was putting the finishing-touches to it himself with a small pot of black paint and a delicate brush. Upon the front of the buck of the tumbril my name went up in a gentle wave, and the address of Silver Ley Farm met it at the crest and led down sinuously across the other side. Above and below and around were gentle flourishes as though the painter had been trying the grace of his curves before beginning, which had miraculously formed a symmetry of soft contours through which the writing meandered like a river. But more; each flourish, thickening in the middle and tailing away, had a grey shadow of itself beside, as though beneath it. As I examined the tumbril I found that edging its square strength were innumerable small decorations, apt as the flower in a yokel's cap—the corner beams were fretted with scallops, and each scallop painted red in contrast to the green of the buck, and there were linings of red here and there, and other evidences of the rough-hewing of its beginning graduating into final moments of exquisite precision. Few indeed, in our days of "fitness for purpose," grow such signs of fancy playing about the feet of toil, the same that led our ancestor to carve his beams and emboss his house-front with a plaster vine.

When Darkie drew that tumbril out of Mark Ashen's yard it was as though a king had departed thence: the wheels resting beside the walls, the old wagons and carts standing waiting for repair, looked joyless, toil-dulled and dilapidated. Even Mark seemed a little older as he turned back from the gate to repair an old shaft.

These things came into my mind as Walter and I greased the wheels of the tumbril whose freshness was hardly worn off though I had had it now several years.

Only the week before I had happened to stop in the little town to call at the butcher's with an order from

Nora. I was not immediately struck by the emptiness
of the Market Hill; the market had died fifty years
ago, and since then the space had been without purpose
except to accommodate the War Memorial, which it
dwarfed. There was not a person in sight, although
it was a bright sunny day with a breeze that looked to
play with flowered frocks. I stopped the trap; and
then I was struck by the fact that the blinds were down
in the shop-windows, not only before the sweets and
haberdashery, for which the sun would have accounted,
but before the cigarettes, the fruit, the stationery. I
thought for a moment I had mistaken the day; but no,
it was not early-closing day. My footfall made me
uneasy by its echo; I found myself being peered at from
the window of the bakery, from an upper window of the
inn; possibly from behind other drawn blinds. I
desisted from my efforts to open the butcher's iron gate,
peered through the lattice above and saw everything
within prepared for business—choice red joints on the
hooks, the block damp and stained, the knife and the
chopper as though just laid down. There was another
door in an alley, which was ajar. I pushed it open and
entered. It was the slaughter-house, cool and dim.
The carcase of a bullock, neatly halved, hung from
roof to floor. Blood was dripping quietly and per-
sistently. A split pig also hung there, and sundry organs
impaled on hooks.

Implements of sinister and unusual curves rested
against the walls—crotched irons, hooks bunched into
claws and enwound by chains like coiled snakes sleeping. Sunlight looked tropically bright through an open
doorway beyond; a blue apron and a pail of water
flashed across. I found an old man through there
swilling out a pig-trough. It was the butcher's father,
very old now and completely under the orders of his
energetic son. I said I had come for a joint of meat,
but——

"A joint—yes, soon now." From the deep pocket of his coarse cord trousers he took out an unexpectedly delicate watch to ascertain the time. This and the replacing of it was gradual as a ceremony, he was so old. "Yes, quite soon." There was a hush in his voice, and it dawned on me that there had been a death, and the shops were all closed for the funeral procession. I asked who. "Mr. Ashen, sir—hadn't you heard?" I shook my head. "He was took very sudden," the old man said in a low voice. We might have been in a church, not a slaughter-house. "Right when he was working. He'd just lifted his hammer, and suddenly he fell down dead. His heart failed him, sir."

The funeral service was in progress at the moment, and this shop, in common with the others along the route where the funeral procession passed to the church and back, was closed for an hour. The old man led the way through into the front shop. "They should soon be coming back now," he said, peering through the lattice. "Yes, here they are." I looked, and saw a thin procession passing into the Market Hill. First a man in a top-hat, then two by two a line of mourners. I knew those men; one saw them daily in shirt-sleeves manipulating the awnings of their shops, scaling ladders, driving horses, digging gardens. But now suddenly I knew them not. It was their clothes, those black suits long laid up, sanctified by a generation of Sundays. Their trousers dented as they walked; their frock coats flapped open, hanging squarely from their high wide shoulders. The older men's beards rested on their chests as they walked with lowered heads; they had an air of quiet purpose, these men who had looked down into the grave and were not far from it themselves, as though they had conferred upon some hard and dutiful matter, an air of wisdom, not of books, but distilled by Time alone, year by patient year, into the eyes, I, too, in the dank and shuttered shop, felt bowed by their occasion.

The procession looked small and lonely, crossing the wide space of blind windows. The bright day was like many children round them; the sunlight flaunting in the square seemed to mock their sombre clothes; the breeze laughed at their solemn pace, plucking at their coats as though to draw them on. But they did not heed the day; the poise of their heads did not alter for sun or wind. They passed slowly. Behind them blinds flew up, shutters swung open. They passed out of sight round the corner, and people came forth again upon the Market Hill. Death had thrust its spoke into the wheel of life. It was withdrawn, and the wheel started again to revolve. A minute ago the town might have been uninhabited; now boots rang on the pavement, shirt-sleeves were being rolled up to the elbows of summer-brown arms. We too stirred; and I became aware again of my surroundings—the twilight studded with a brilliant constellation where the lattice was, the red joints around, the odour of flesh, and the knives. The old man folded back the shutters, and the deathly cavern brightened into a butcher's shop. The subdued tone of voice was gone too; he seemed years younger as he enquired my needs in the brisk and cheerful voice of business.

As I drove away there were yet a few dark figures among the bright print frocks of summer; in an open cottage door a woman was slipping a white pinafore over a dress of black alpaca. But Mark Ashen's premises did not re-awaken; no window opened, no blind lifted. His gates were shut; I had never seen them so since I had lived in this place. Within, the yard was empty, the forge black.

Later his name was taken down from over the threshold, and a "For Sale" board substituted. The yard was cleared of cart, cart-wheel, and every sign of his trade. Nobody came to carry on the business of Mark Ashen.

The country seemed to besiege that small town which had once been as important as the size of its church testified; Time eroded it slowly back to a village. It was a community founded upon individuality; each of its needs had once been supplied by one of its citizens. I reflected on these things at the vanishing of one more of its individual trades—that of the wheelwright. Older men have told me of the notables of their youth when there was still a weekly market on Market Hill, each living modestly on the proceeds of one occupation. Is this the age of specialisation? There used to be one whose whole trade was the selling of tea. Another used to be a cheesemonger and travelled over the country sampling and buying cheeses, which he brought back to his home town, where he was patronised by all the farmers, whose taste in cheese, as in meat, is exacting. "You can't get cheeses like that nowadays," old men tell their sons. Now a multiple stores has jammed a flashy window into an old building, and embraces these trades and many others under one roof. The window is filled mainly with tins and cardboard effigies of smiling health. Cheese is just cheese, plastic, geometrical.

I have had many glimpses of the life of the little town amid its encircling cornfields at all hours. It is in the mellow years of old age; it has retired from business to cultivate its garden; that is the impression it gives. The country even sits upon its roofs in moss and lichen, and upon its walls in wallflowers, and in grass between its paving-stones.

Sometimes a Latin appears as from nowhere with barrel-organ and monkey, flashing a smile at the children he draws dancing after him, while his harassed-looking wife with a baby at her breast shuffles hurriedly cap-in-hand from door to door. Modern tunes go shouting into all its alleys and get no answer; old-age pensioners stand and peer. The children follow as far as the last lamp-post, and then turn back reluctant to their pavement play.

At harvest-time the loads pass through, and a few car-loads of explorers stop and look and call it a discovery. But mostly its flow of life is local. Its traffic varies with the hours. In the early morning there is first a secret and multitudinous patter, which to those who have half an eye awake enough to see is the passing of a herd of cows. And later, about such time as the shopkeepers are sweeping each his piece of pavement and mats are being shaken in doorways, the milk come jingling to town in that kind of cart which derives from the ancient chariot. And just as its citizens are pouring that milk into their breakfast tea, the cows pass by again to the meadows which are at the end of the street, where it turns into a country road.

During the morning there is a certain bustle occasioned by the provisioning of the houses for the day. The policeman, at some period, marches as far as the last lamp-post, where he pauses to see if there is any likelihood of a vehicle from the side road coinciding with one going along the street, in which case he will stay the one with uplifted hand and wave on the other.

From one till two the shops close, but actually by half-past twelve a kind of second sleep has fallen on the town, so that a prowling cat looks somehow furtive and significant; and not till toward three is business to any extent resumed.

As sundown approaches, its main street grows briefly lively and light-hearted. Men and girls released from different work—labourers, silk-weavers, shop-assistants —pass by on bicycles toward their country homes, their faces aglow in the deepening light, speeding along as though life were all free-wheel. Then the traffic abates again, and the sun has the street to itself along which to set. On the pavements it is the hour of doorway chat. Pipe smoke evaporates like the threads of talk.

Now those for whom the street seems to wait in its flush of evening begin to appear at its far end. The dogs, if ever they barked at them, do so no longer, for they are a daily occurrence, one which the people smoking in doorways seldom pause in their conversation to observe. The tramps are coming to town.

They are like the first stragglers of a defeated army, these for whom the sun gold-paves the street in mock triumph. In their faces, bearing, gait, one seems to read the fortunes of their ill-starred day. They have, somehow, a disturbing effect, for all the citizens' studied indifference to them, as though their coming presaged the end of the security of those who sit comfortably here in houses and walled gardens.

They look neither to right nor left, but mostly in the gutter, where sometimes one finds something of value to him. There is a subtle but distinct difference between the professional tramps and the others. The former are worn down to a uniformity; they have the listlessness of automata; usually one shoulder is carried higher than the other through being long humped with a burden; their legs have a loose, flinging gait, as though composed solely of the flapping trousers. But the others wear their solitude as though it were a suit of mourning. They walk stiffly, as though every window were jeering, "Welcome, freemen of the city!" And on their faces, as they come nearer, in their eyes, is the reflection of the battle they have lost. Their expressions are still a conflict between that best of them which would have graced good fortune, and that which has brought them low.

At the corner where they turn to go to the workhouse they stop, and, stooping down, open their bundles and put things into them from their pockets, or vice versa. One is sewing something into the lining of his coat. Then, having arranged their possessions to their satisfaction, they continue to where the workhouse gates stand open to receive them.

The tide of men is all down-street at this hour of evening; only one goes against it, as ragged as they, but carrying his cap in his hand. He walks a few paces, pauses, and looks at the upper windows, then walks slowly on again. He is singing. The notes are clear though wavering. The street now is quiet as a ravine to his song; none of the windows comes alive. One door opens, though, and a woman looks out with a coin in her hand. But he has already gone past; slowly as he travels, he has been a little too quick for his moment of good fortune. His back continues toward the half-offered coin, which he step by step leaves behind.

He walks on singing in the face of the sun, against the tide of those whose backs are toward it. His voice is the last hope of the emptying street at nightfall. It lingers long between echoing walls like the dying light.

CHAPTER XIII

IN edging his most prosaic handiwork with those touches of toy-like decoration, the local craftsman shows himself true to his nature as a reflection of the earth's. I found in it a power of co-ordination, unconscious very likely, as the tumbril toiled loaded over the stubble-field. For pimpernel and late poppy made gay the stark ground even as in spring its bare harrowed earth was edged with oxlips all round the hedge. Such minutiæ of beauty ever compensate the huge uncouthness of husbandry, whose rough shoulder is continually rubbing them. As for the stiff coat of the working man, one day it is snow upon its lapels and another blossoms, and the stolid purpose pushes on through all. Thus is man in his first and ultimate environment. A balance of the coarse and fine may be dimly apprehended here, which grows into a nobility hard to define the more it is observed.

Between post and lintel of the stable-door, early morning displayed for me a cobweb hung with dew. And so it was through the day, and my work in its pauses was inwardly exhilarated by the light of such delicate things. Maybe one needed some such symbols for the co-ordination of fineness and roughness in personal nature. Here one had it completely, like water sparkling to the lips of a man thirst-distracted from his wholeness of being. It was a surety of sensation beyond the compass of words, so I will not attempt anything further upon it, save to remark that Nora had the quicker eye for the toys and phantom-corners of Nature, and they leavened work to the winsomeness of play.

When she pointed to a fleck of dark fluff floating across the pond I dismissed it as a piece of soiled thistle-down, and would have turned away but that she cried it was alive.

A closer look revealed that it was a baby moorhen energetically exploring the element into which it had been born, though it appeared rather as though it were being blown along by consecutive gusts of wind. Seeing us eyeing it, the parent birds came forth from the watery cavern which leafy boughs had made of their nesting-place, and took up positions on either side of their infant, uttering warning noises and jerking their tails in their clockwork fashion. They accompanied it as a convoy; but at length it made directly over towards where we stood, and even parental solicitude would not dare venture farther than half-way across. There they stayed rowing up and down in a frenzy of anxiety, clucking the most fearful forebodings, to which the impudent fluff-ball paid not the least attention. It came almost to our feet, explored a little along the bank and returned in a leisurely manner to its parents, asking, I think, what all the fuss was about seeing that we were so demonstrably harmless.

We looked for others, but there were none. Remembering the spring labours of the parent birds we found it analogous to the fable of the mountain and the mouse that this "tiny mite o' thing," as Nora quoted from Walter's idiom, should be the sole result.

Altogether they had built three nests, two at the far end of the pond and one quite near the house. Strange to say, it was the near one that they used at last. Nora called to me one day to witness the zeal of the moorhen as a home-builder, for one of them was attempting to drag a piece of plank, quite four inches wide and a foot long, across the water to their hole. It was in a frantic state of determination, so that it did not notice us watching from the bank. It just managed to nip a corner of the plank with its beak, and struggled forward with head averted, pulling the wood along beside it. Every yard the plank slipped from its beak and it had to take a fresh hold. Halfway home it tried another method. Remaining motionless in the water, it attempted to lever the plank along with movements of its beak. When the plank had floated beyond it, it swam forward to the front end and repeated the process. Thus, half carrying, half pushing, it drew its trophy home into the sandy cave at last, but immediately reappeared and swam quickly across the pond again, returning laboriously with another piece of wood only slightly smaller than the first.

The two birds showed extreme anxiety for their single offspring, though it seemed almost too small, too light for harm. If it were out alone in mid-pond for more than a few minutes, one or other would come fussing after, and escort it, ruffling the glassy surface as a figure-skater scores his movements upon the ice. The youngster grew his feathers, and one day there had arrived that red splash upon the front of his head as though dropped from the sky. Then suddenly the two parents flew away, and left him alone on the pond.

But he seems always too busy to notice that they were ever there or ever went, walking tilted forward, peering everywhere with his elastic neck, like an industrious shopper pecking with covetousness at plate-glass windows. A flitting creature, preoccupied with the things beneath, earth and water, whose tail seems to lead a separate, St. Vitus life of its own. He hates the larger air of other birds; he hates to fly except when startled. Then it is as though the stilled twilight jumped in its first sleep—his panic cry and trailing legs scoring the solid calm of the pool like a sudden crack running across a mirror—and the sunset sways there, and the reflected boughs weave themselves, long after the rest of the place has forgotten the voice. It is a shriek of that sharp dolour of watery stretches, of a desolation which the owl's hoot has not for all its wildness, for the owl's is a wood-note echoing the confinement of thickets, the note of Pan.

The plover also visits our homely husbandry with a cry of other worlds. Above the gusty knoll in early spring, when our scarecrow guards the sown earth, turning with wide-flung arms this way, that way, as though to shake off the importuning wind; before an arras of storm-cloud deep as the violets that shake under the bleak thorns, the plovers, like two black butterflies, twist and fall, weaving their weird love-flight, mewing of desolation.

But above them is the lark—even though the cloud spreads over like dusk and turns him to a bat—re-assuring the earth with his song. It is of the sun when the sun were by any other means unimaginable. And other birds—thrushes, blackbirds—sing to one another through the gale from the shelter of garden walls, from the leafy ilex and their hedgerow fastnesses. "Still here, here," they cry.

The voice of the cow answering with low reassurance the wail of her calf is from the very heart of maternal solicitude, all defensive, fearful to save. But the horse when he neighs, throwing up his head, defying the bridle, distending his nostrils, is not a generation distant from him that "smelleth the battle from afar." His neigh forgets the harness; it is the wild trumpet of his strength. It is like cock-crow, that shakes the whole frame and every plume of the bird. The cock seems to put forth all his strength in his call, then claps his wings and looks about him as though telling himself, "That was fine." The hen only murmurs to herself of the mysterious feelings stirring within her.

The voices of the farm and its fields are the choir of life—the vaunt, the secret murmur, the bright cheer —the plover whirling down as from a gunshot with his death-cry, the lark in the same sky undaunted— from the deep low of the cow to the squeak of the bat, the pipistrelle, which is like the chink of the smallest chain in the world, all chanting around and above the thoughtful silence of man, as he turns their instincts and ecstasies to his own uses. Yet he cannot but feel himself part of the same inscrutable destiny as is theirs he lives among. The fate that is both luring, ruth-less, and relenting, is his and theirs. He is to his beasts the power of the unforeseen which tyrannises over him. There is Fortune's smile which too impetuously greeted turns into a frown; there are winds that search through field and yard; there is the iron command of daily labour; but there is a warm corner in the straw pen, there is a warm hearth-side hour. The morrow impends inscrutably over all.

But of all the voices I think I like most the sparrows'. They are companionable, with their chirrup-chirrup-chirrup; they do not wait on weather or season; the coldest day or the drowsiest they chatter away on eaves and straw and hedges; they fill the whole country with childish life, and the more man's hand is against them the more they seem to visit him in merry multitudes. Being a farmer, I poison them; Walter destroys their nests; the cats stalk them; but they are always there.

In the village school there was a picture of St. Francis and the birds—a kind of educational poster-picture pinned to the wall. I wondered what the authorities desired its message to be. For, as I walked in to call the roll one day, I heard a boy being reprimanded for gazing on this picture instead of attending to what the mistress was trying to teach him. His punishment was to be that he stood before the picture during the following play-time. School ended in a week, and he was leaving school then and going to work for Bob Chilgrove. I happened to be talking to Bob Chilgrove in his yard the day the boy Jack started to work for him. Bob was discussing wheat prices.

"Over-production everywhere," he said, "that's what's the matter. Do you know, yesterday I met a chap who'd just come back after trying to make a living in Canada; he said he was offered sixpence a bushel for his wheat, and rather than sell it at that price he burnt it where it stood—his whole crop——

"Look at them damned old sparrows. I reckon there's a thousand on that stack, eating the corn. Shoo! Hi, Jack! Jack! . . .

"Yes, he set fire to it rather than sell it at that. . . .

"Oh, Jack, did you soak that peck of wheat in the poison as I told you?"

"Yes, sir, here it be."

"Well, you might lay it along all the gutterings of the barn; we must get rid of these sparrows—they eat all the corn. . . . Yes, over-production," he repeated, "that's the trouble to-day."

The next day I saw Jack collecting bunches of dead sparrows and burying them.

I am still uncertain as to the intended message of the picture on the schoolroom wall.

The cycling draper, that indefatigable talker and pedaller, paid us yet another visit. His white beard parted in the middle and had a tendency to curve away to either side as though through the force with which he met the wind as he travelled along. It gave him at any rate a breezy appearance, and the optimism with which he persisted in his calls was, or should have been, according to those advertisements relating to salesmanship, one of the ingredients of success.

Was there anything we might be wanting this morning?
He enumerated socks, ties, handkerchiefs (ladies' and
gents'), stockings, etc., etc., in the confident tone of
one bringing coveted necessaries to dwellers in year-
long isolation. Politely we intimated that, as though
by a coincidence, we happened to be well supplied
with just those very things he mentioned.

"Ah, well," he said, "I like to give you a call—in
case."

We intimated our appreciation. "Just to see how
you're getting on," he added.

But it did not end there. He was seventy-six, and
had a shop in the next village but one. Until the age
of sixty he used to tricycle, but then learnt to bicycle.
He found it, he said, "more expeditious." He used
to have a shop at the other end of the county, but he
was burnt out. He swept his arm about his head to
indicate the spectacular proportions of the blaze.
"Thatched roof, you know. But it can't happen to
me like that again; I've got a tin roof this time." He
twinkled at us, and we duly applauded his foresight.
"We learn by experience," he said. "You don't get
anywhere in life, else." It was not quite clear where
he had "got," but he was still young to his ambition.
We asked him how the fire happened. "Traction-
engine," he said. "Sparks." He continued, "I lived
on a hill, and the engine had a great load on it, and it
puffed. Lord, it puffed up that hill"—he worked his
clenched fists before him like pistons—"chuff—chuff—
chuff. The sparks flew out of the funnel like a fire-
work. Chuff! Right on to my roof." He gave a
robust representation of the whole proceeding. A
power of a man he seemed, but one had an inkling that
maybe much was allowed to escape in the steam of
exuberance.

But there was no doubt in his mind that he was in
a considerable way of business. "It was a long time

before I found just the place to suit me after that. Then I came to this part. But next they wanted to sell my place along with the whole row of cottages. I turned round and bought the lot," he said; "the whole lot."

He added, "They were all let but one, and I had an offer of half a crown a week for that. I was just going to accept when a London man retiring from business offered me three shillings. Of course, I snapped at it."

"Of course," we echoed.

"Well, I'll bid you good day for this morning," he said. "I'll give you a call next week."

"Thank you," we said, as though to the family doctor, for somehow he had the air of stopping just to see that all was well with us; and away he went, planting one foot on the step of his bicycle, pushing it off before him with three great hops, mounting in that agile-elderly manner of a spring over the back of the saddle.

But we could not let him always draw blank, even after we had discovered what his black suitcase contained. This we discovered the third time he called, for he was so sorry he had missed us the week before (we had been out) that we felt we really ought to need something he supplied. Nora suddenly bethought her, "You do need a few more handkerchiefs."

The suitcase was off his handlebars in a twinkling, and he opened it on the kitchen table. I presume the outside was black the more to contrast with the brilliance of the contents.

"Er—really, Nora, you need stockings more than I need handkerchiefs," I suggested, my eye travelling from the red, spotted corner to the shrimp-pink.

"No, I have plenty of stockings," said Nora, treading firmly upon my toe under the table.

"Never heard a lady say that before," chimed in the draper's ready wit; but he was already displaying the handkerchiefs. They were of every colour but

white, bold as the late Mark Ashen's newly painted
carts, flowery as the prime.

I chose two mock-Paisley and a passionate purple.
"I shall wear them whenever I go to town," I assured
him and threatened her.

We were thrashing; and then I was going to cut
up the straw into chaff, as it was fine long golden straw
which had ripened early and escaped by a day the
subsequent downpours. It lay in its mazy freshness
as flung from the elevator, whose continuous teeth
curtained it down upon the stack, where it piled till one
of us brushed it aside with a fork and stood on it,
stamping it in. Walter was building the straw-stack,
but the straw was so light that when he stood and
jerked his weight down on it, to make firm a corner,
the whole stack shook like a sprung mattress.

I had hired Bob Chilgrove's thrashing tackle along
with some of his men. He could not get on at all for
the wet state of the ground, so he had let me have the
tackle, as my last year's oats had hardly lasted out,
owing to Kitty's extra mouth to feed. Not only that
either, but I suspected that robberies of the granary
by Walter had depleted the stock. It was pride that
induced Walter to steal from me to give to mine, for
the horses were his responsibility. There is a certain
standard at which a horse may be kept well and fit
for any work of the farm. But there is above that a
superfluous fitness, which turns a strong rough plough-
horse into a king of power—it puts a shine upon his
coat and a plumpness upon his haunches, gives him a
patrician air of condescension to his task. He seems
to vaunt himself in every movement and compels the
notice of the passer-by.

Little by little I had found that Captain and Dewdrop were becoming a lion hearted pair. It began
with the breaking-in of Captain as a colt. "We must

feed him well seeing he's new to the work," Walter said, and I agreed, as Captain was put to work that a newly broken colt is not usually asked to perform, on account of the exigencies of the season. On almost every farm there is a guerilla struggle continually in progress between the farmer and the horse-keeper over the horse-corn, the farmer allotting two bushels per week to each working animal, and watching while the horse-keeper and a ploughman put it up in sacks. The horse-keeper piles the bushel measure as high as it will hold, and fills each sack till there hardly seems room to tie up the mouth. He punches the shoulders of the sack to bring the mouth within compass of his hand, while his mate puts the string round it. Even then a good-humoured argument is begun. "That don't weigh twelve stone, master." "I know it do— and more." "Nay, look ye, they oats be wonderful light; half on 'em ain't no better'n chaff." And for the nth time the oats are poured from hand to hand and examined under the light of a glass tile in the roof. The sacks are carried into the stable and the farmer turns the key with a clatter in the lock and—puts it in his pocket? No, hangs it on a nail round the corner! But it is enough; it is a sign that the door is locked and not to be opened without permission.

I had relaxed the rule in favour of the colt, and had in the beginning virtually condoned Walter's "slipping" into the granary with a scoop for a little extra for Captain, and later had not come to frowning on it, though the colt was a horse now and it was apparent that Dewdrop had also benefited.

Nor was it unnoticed outside the farm. Journeys to market and jobs on road-side fields led to me being hailed in the market and Walter in the inn with, "Your horses are as fat as butter."

This made Walter mantle with pleasure and smile into his beer, for it was the top of every horse-keeper's ambition to walk beside the almost decadent splendour of a pair of dainty-legged, plump-bodied Suffolks, just as another may long for an eight-cylinder limousine, though a four-cylinder tourer accomplishes the same journey.

But on my side this excess of well-being was something to be explained away, or otherwise accounted for. The implication was not, "How good to have such horses," but "How your horse-keeper hoodwinks you!"

The result was, we were short of corn and chaff and had to thrash as soon as we had reaped. The restrictions should return to force over the new oats. For, though I enjoyed it, the extra sheen and grandeur was a luxury of the eyes which modern farmers could ill afford. If only one were rich enough to pamper one's beasts into living sculpture! To riot in all those complex rations which the books recommend!

We were short-handed on the straw-stack; it became far across, and there was nobody to come between Walter and me and pass the straw over. The Danaæan shower never ceased; the machinery poured it out relentlessly, and one's work resolved itself hour by hour into a struggle to master it, to get it away before it piled up and choked its source. For that would stop the machines, and the machines would stop every man. They worked, the men, in a rhythmic co-ordination round the machines; their movements were bound to the time of the wheels, and the beaters that were like the agitated throat of a wooden idol vomiting the golden straw. Its speech was the sharp tearing groan as each sheaf was drawn in, smashed, devoured by its man-devised digestive organism.

The smooth motion of the wheels and the puffs of the engine beating the roar into a primitive syncopation, kept the work to its pace. A pile of straw fell on the heap that my fork was just going to shift, weighting it like lead. It will not move now, my arms cry, aching already, and slacken helplessly. But it must be moved, says the will, for the beaters are beating more out every moment, and the machine is the master of the moment, my mind his overseer, my arms his slaves. Necessity braces them: they heave, they cry mercy, they get none; the pile shifts slowly, rolls and trails on my bending fork to Walter; his fork transfixes it; its weight dies like the wind; I turn again; another pile stands in its place, even as a man on the corn-stack takes a second more determined heave at a mat of sheaves that resist his power.

Then a rat runs across the stack down there; the work rhythm is broken by three men; with quick, spontaneous movements they pursue it; eagerness burns in their eyes. The rest of us work on, but our eyes find release in the little group bending together in play, in laughter. Their truancy has turned their forks into weapons; they are armed men; they jab and thrust and scuffle with their feet in a corner. Suddenly they slacken apart; one lifts the rat impaled on a tine and flings him over the hedge. It is done; their bodies droop, and the intentness dies from their eyes as they return and take up again the regular swing of the work.

Only the dog, his tail wagging erect as he burrows deep in the sheaves after other rats, keeps the plume of sport flying.

That not all the traditional joviality among labourers is dead, as some assert, was evident as we were chaff-cutting after the thrashing. We were filling the chaff-barn, but Walter was filling the small chaff-house next the stable, which was some distance away across the yard slippery with mud. While he was gone with a bag, I saw one of the other men come with three large mangolds, another pick up two drain-pipes, a third collect a number of old ploughshares. These with many smiles and winks they tipped into the bag that was filling, gathering yet more till the bag was weighted down, though to feel the outside of it it contained only chaff. They laid it ready for Walter, and as he approached their smiles died away, and they assumed a serious preoccupation with their work, while covertly watching him and sharing the relish of his first fruitless hoist at the bag. He tried again, lifted it to his shoulders, and started off. The slippery ground caused his feet to stagger, and the sack dragged down his back, making its true weight felt. Something dawned on him as he made uncertain, bent progress like an overloaded ant. He turned, and found everybody in roars of laughter. "Ha! I thought there were something more'n chaff in this," he cried, but being midway across, had to continue the whole distance.

But he took it in good part, being cheered by a recent piece of good fortune when we had thrashed the stack. For while loading in the harvest-field he had lost the watch from his waistcoat pocket. One would expect a workman to have a turnip watch, but very often the reverse is the case, and it is some small silver heirloom with its key hanging beside it that is produced from the corduroy pocket when you ask the time.

Walter's was one of this kind. He searched the field in vain; we watched as we unloaded the sheaves, and when hope had been given up, the watch fell out of a sheaf at the bottom of the stack as it was being lifted on to the drum.

I have also known a watch lost during harvest to be found again the following spring, when the stack came to be thrashed.

CHAPTER XIV

Now the gipsies came, a slant-eyed, weather-beaten crew, flamboyant and lank like the very over-ripeness of summer. Whether they ever were that proud type of the flowing savage that some writers have supposed, or inwardly still are, they showed little sign of it. They looked furtive and suspicious by day as they dragged through our lanes towards the small town which was the scene of one of the last of their summer fairs. The main show went by towards afternoon, traction engines fantastically gilded and huge vans, even motor-lorries, bedizened with the sinuous flourish of nomadism. These proclaimed George Jessel's Steam Galloping Horses. They had only that one pace, presumably. There were also the same gentleman's Celebrated Amusements. Followed a caravan that might have been the coronation coach of the Great Cham of Tartary, and others, lesser, but glistering, as of the princes of the blood royal. After that, the shabby nags and ragged-looking conveyances which followed gave the impression of a once splendid people fallen on evil days; for even the worst, the most tarpaulin substitute for a caravan, had stuck about it a brass spiral or two, and a door with a crystal handle and a mirror for a finger-plate. And these, though the roof was smoke-blackened and every utensil filthy, were polished to diamonds and twisted ribbons of sunlight.

There were one or two places on the road where i

was feared some might camp, and our policeman was vigilant in keeping them moving. Bob Chilgrove stood at his farm gate with his stick and two dogs, watching them by; Joe Boxted the same, though what they would have cared to steal from his place one could not imagine.

Everybody was out to guard his own and see that they did not loiter near his premises. Mothers called their children to them from the road, out of contact with the gipsies' children, cottagers' dogs barked at their dogs till their kennels shook; but their dogs, like their masters, slouched by without reply. The road became a ravine through which this gaudy people were given passage as through a hostile land. Nearly always the labourer at the roadside hedge, the cottager in his garden, will unbend at a passing footstep, stretch, lean on his tool, and pass the time of day. He paused now, turned and met the gipsies eye to eye, but spoke no word.

The countryman, anchored to his plot of land and working for his own provision, instinctively distrusts all that is volatile, unsettled, passing with the moment. The gipsies go by like dreams out of the night of his unfulfilled being, the urge of roystering youth on which his daytime nature flung the earth of prudence, again and again, till those hours are just such a rabble as this, furtive in the finery of braggadocio.

These are of the night, of the flame-hour—they are hectic by night, but drab and shamed-looking by day. By night, too, the countryman, having put up his spade, forgets his daytime self; he is lured by the phœnix of the fair, lured to lose himself in the shadows of the flickering lights, to be hypnotised by the roar and the rhythm.

Sometimes an old Medusa, with snaky, hanging hair, squatted on the front of a caravan, driving with one hand and clutching a child with the other; sometimes a young girl with bare legs and feet dangling sideways held the reins. On one, a young man with curling lips and hair lolled like a prince in scorn. He insulted the policeman with his bold, silent stare; his woman had black arching brows, and wore a paper flower at her breast and red piping on her high boots.

I passed them camped that night just outside Benfield. Several men stood a little away from a fire whose leaping lights fawned wolfishly upon them, hollowing their cheeks and eyes; the young man lolled on his elbow close before the fire, which rosily blandished him, petting his forehead, cheeks, and arms like a courtesan.

The parsonage meadow was pavilioned with vast tarpaulins, whose angular, incomplete shapes suggested gigantic women dressing under their night-gowns. Hammering and shouting continued far into the night: the inhabitants, strolling after tea, observed it all cautiously from a distance. Those men and their shouting haste were very foreign to them.

Next night the tarpaulins were off; with a great blare and glitter the fair announced itself, and Benfield and the surrounding villages walked in.

Reuben Russet's farmhouse adjoined the parsonage meadow: as we passed we saw his door open, and he cried to us from within. We joined the number that already filled the wide, low room. Reuben was large and patient, with slow, trusty eyes like a horse. His head missed the beams of the ceiling by an inch. As he stood there leaning his arm on one he seemed to be holding the whole ceiling up. His wife was small and fiery-haired. Reuben stood amid a flock of brothers and sisters-in-law sitting at the long table at tea. He stood leaning against the beam to welcome us, and I thought he looked tired through his smile, for he bore a heavy yoke of labour in trying to keep solvent. His brothers had been farming during the war; Reuben had been fighting. He milked and delivered the milk daily—having started with a few gallons on the handle-bars of a pedal-cycle. Now he had a big round. Also he did a great deal of work on the farm. This evening he wanted just to sit in his porch, I think, and puff at his pipe. But the clang and trumpeting of the fair sounded like the cymbals of some ritual dance, and stirred the others.

"Reuben's going to take me on the swings in a minute," cried his wife. "He's got to swing me right up to the beam."

"There, you see what you have to do when you get caught by one of them," he smiled at me, and jerked back his thumb.

"What!" cried his wife in mock outrage. "Caught! I like that. If you didn't come fifty miles every week-end after me."

"Ah, there's no knowing what you'll do when you're young and foolish." He smiled indolently out over the fields, tapping the brick floor absent-mindedly with his boot.

She threw a radish at him. Suddenly he turned and caught her by the wrists. She struggled, laughing and flinging defiance up at him and shaking her red hair; then suddenly she cried, "Oh, you brute!" and fell slack and helpless against him like a wilted flower. He smiled down at her tenderly, though his hands remained tight round her wrists. "Come on, then," he said.

Chairs scraped, and we got up. His father was in the room, and he remained, and Bob Chilgrove would have done, only his wife chivied him up. He looked at the fair dubiously. "Don't know as I want to go among that crowd," he said.

But she hauled him out. Major Russet, however, stayed behind, having a telegraphic conversation with his father consisting of a word or two and a long silence,

possibly full of meaning for those in the know. Old
Russet was often to be found up at Reuben's farm.
For the old man, though he had retired from farming
to a house in the village, could not rest out of it. The
house had a square, imposing front; a car stood in the
garage, and there was a chauffeur-gardener who looked
after it. When the old man went out of the front door,
it was in the genteel and dignified manner of one who is
deservedly resting on his laurels, while the chauffeur
held open the door of his car. But more often he
would slip out of the back door in an old coat and cap
and over the fields to where Reuben was working, and
all morning he would be steering the corn-drill for him
or burning hedge-trimmings. That was where he
was happiest. He could not rest for thinking of what
Reuben might be doing that day.

"He said he didn't think that field would be dry
enough to harrow—but it would be this afternoon.
I wonder if he's at it."

As we went on down to the fair, Reuben said to
me, "Did you hear what mother said at the pictures
the other day? Major took her and father into Stambury
to them because she's never been to a cinema before—
let alone a talkie. There was a big film on—*Ben Hur*
—thousands of people in it. She said, 'Wherever are
all them people going to find room to sleep in Stambury
to-night?' They told her they weren't real people, only
photographs. She said, 'They must be real people; I can
hear them talking.'"

We lost ourselves and each other among the crowds
in the fair. The old familiarity of the people was
somehow transformed—they were both strangers and
friends; strangers to those sober selves of the day, yet
friends of the moment of running against one another,
of the laughter of the roundabout. One knew nobody,
and yet in a sense one knew everybody. Flame and
music were the elixir. The gipsies flared beside their

stalls. Gone now the drooping, resentful shuffle. They
flung off their outlawry, or rather they lured the
villagers to share it. Darkness was the cave of their
witchery. In the flame-light the girls brandished balls
before the cokernut shies, offered them with a shout
and flash of gold rings, like Borgia apples. One caught
them in bold attitudes, as of a Spanish dance. The
young villagers laughed and joked with them now, and
vied with each other before them.

All around stood the still trees, their nearest boughs
just dipping in the light. I walked aside there, alone,
out of it. Cock pheasants cackled in alarm; a white
owl floated away. All Nature was uneasy to-night.
The fair was like a drunken man alone in a cathedral;
it reeled and laughed up at the austere starlight. The
bell which great strength rang sounded at long intervals
like a harsh knell, and in between the demoniac whoops
of the roundabout. The rhythm of the organ-tunes
was as though carved out of wood. Heart-beats of
the paste-board Babylon. I was drawn back to it,
unreasonably exhilarated by the laughter bursting out
like wind-swayed flowers under the night-shade. I
was put in mind of great things I had once planned to
do; how all my strength was to have been poured out in
wrestling with angels of the difficult beauty of words,
and instead, how careful I had grown in day-to-day
cultivation of the earth, how content with felicity and
shrunken in ambition.

But now for a moment I was caught up (however
such blare and blatancy had the power) by the old
desire, the old fever which could burn up every earthly
consideration.

As I walked through those glistering arcades at
midnight, in which the pounding music turned the
reality of people into a mime of puppets, I was excited
again by the dream that there was something in life
which I alone knew, which I alone must tell.

THE CHERRY TREE

The roundabout was the heart of the fair, a swirl of light, a vortex to which everyone was drawn. Its architecture looked like the racked ghost or second childhood of the Louis Quatorze. Ruskin would have called the painted figures which adorned it extreme examples of the Ignoble Grotesque. Kings and queens stood on the pinnacles of the steam organ, vibrating to the music. Heroes of the Boer War—at least, two of them bore a distinct moustache likeness to Lord Roberts and Lord Kitchener—stood to rigorous attention on the brass spirals. Snaking itself round the top was a multi-coloured announcement which made me sure, for a moment, that I had strayed into the world of Daisy Ashford's *Young Visiters*—"Patronised by His Majesty." Until, going closer, I discerned a minute apostrophe S and the word "subjects."

Bob Chilgrove was carrying his wife pillion on one of the "galloping horses," which, but for the fine frenzy of its eye and nostril, would have provided a fair parody of the old-style farmer's market journey. But that was not the mount to do a "butter and eggs" trot. Bob's dubiousness was gone since he had found himself riding next to a neighbour farmer. He was laughing broadly and recapturing his youth. It was a weird unwearying cavalcade of palfreys and monstrous chanticleers, of pointed shoes, shivering skirts, red hands clasping satin waists, all journeying to nowhere.

Reuben, meanwhile, was doing his duty nobly on the swing-boats. They swung like giant pendulums, like those in a clock-maker's dream—all at sixes and sevens. He heaved on the plush rope, standing up to it and swinging his small wife a complete half-circle. The steep downward glide dazzled her, sent her bobbed hair rushing free through the air.

I was even tempted into the fortune-teller's grot. It was somehow an hour of fate, all care being blotted out with the landscape we tended, the avenues of life we had not chosen opening out once again before us, beckoning. Many flaps and curtains seemed to close behind me as I entered, till the fair even grew faint, and I sat in a hot thrumming privacy with the gipsy who wore a paper flower, and red piping on her boots. She had hooded herself with a dark veil. I laid my hand, as she commanded, palm uppermost upon the velvet-covered table, and she traced the many little lines of it, and composed on them until they became roads through a strange land, dangerously intersected, alluringly vagrant. To think that all my fortune lay in that little declivity! And there my life-line ran over the brink into nothingness, running away like water even as one tries to catch it to the lips.

I was of an adventurous, uncertain disposition, she told me; there was a dark woman in my life; there were also tears on account of me by a fair woman. "Any more?" I asked; but she frowned and looked intent. I should handle money, I should have much money—but I should spend it all.

When was I born? October the fourth, I told her. Ah, then, that accounted for my very perplexing nature, for September was a careful month, October was a wild reckless month, and my life was a conflict between the two, sometimes too prudent, almost miserly, at others spending like water.

So out again into the night with my personality thus fortified, into the scintillation and music and interweaving of people's shadows over the lank bruised grass. My spendthrift future was like heady wine, and the dark lady and the fair lady who wept, and this flattering conflict of the elements in me.

The traction-engines that worked all the side-shows stood together in a corner, like benign monsters enjoying a chat and a puff. The engine's rôle to the agricultural labourer is usually that of taskmaster. At six in the morning its whistle summons him to his post

by the thrashing-machine in the semi-darkness, and its
fierce jets start the inexorable wheels revolving. But
now it was harnessed to serve his pleasures—a complete
social revolution.

"Sin and Scandal of the Smart Set Revealed"
announces a booth. Is it that one will really learn
at last of that mysterious clique whose luxurious but
miserably harassed lives are the anxiety of every
novelette-reader? It is worth risking a penny on it,
even should it destroy one more castle in Spain of
daring and devil-may-care. The revelation comes by
the insertion of a penny in a slot, the application of
the eyes to an aperture, and the turning of a handle.

A middle-aged labourer is at the moment conducting
an investigation, while his wife and children stand by.
The bent back gives no clue to his feelings. "What can
you see, Alf?" asks his wife at last. "I can't see
nothin'," he grumbles. "Do you have a look." She
hands him the baby and applies herself to the machine.

"There's somethin' movin' in there," is all she can
make out.

"Huh!" says the man. They give it up and move
on, still knowing no more of the life of the "gentry"
than can be seen from the gates of their parks.

Nevertheless, it is difficult to resist a pennyworth.
My coin started a dim, brief cinema in the machine.
It seemed to consist chiefly in an artist (identification,
a bow-tie) paying more attention to his slightly swathed
model than to his art. I was stooping with my eyes
clamped to the thing, like a professional photographer,
when I received a poke in the back. It was Nora.

"Just where you would be found," she said.

"Never mind, I'll get you a cokernut," I offered, and
we went off to the nearest shy. Young men were
flinging with a vigour which jerked their coats half
off their shoulders, while a gipsy girl incited them to
fresh efforts against the phlegmatic bearded cokernuts

ranged in rows like traitors' heads on the Tower. The balls bounced far and wide, beating a tattoo to the music. We broke one and dislodged another; but I will not say that either was cheap.

"Now a packet of cigarettes," I volunteered, and took up a weapon at the rifle range. One shot corks at the packets set on end. A brief inspection showed that the sights were falsified, but by looking along the barrel I managed to hit a packet full in the middle three times out of three. It quivered but did not fall.

"By gum," cried a youthful admirer of my aim. I was inclined to agree with him.

Along the flaring alley-ways young men were teasing their girls with every device of surprise that was to be bought there, or adorning them with paper feathers. By contrast, the breeze lifted a tent-flap, and like a cynic wit revealed two men in shirt-sleeves eating bread and cheese on a soap-box in gloomy silence. Perhaps they were thinking of the huge labour of putting up the fair yesterday, and the huge labour of pulling it all down again to-morrow. For the showmen there was perhaps a communicated glamour as they stood and shouted in the light—but for the engineers in shadowy corners, none.

It was time to be thinking of home, of returning to our native simplicity and silence. But first there was a choice of wonders. "The Headless Egyptian" or "The Smallest Horse in the World." There was a time when the first would have commanded the greater crowd, but that time is past. The village is growing up. Several from Benfield served in Egypt during the war, and their opinion of it, given out in the Cock Inn, was to the effect that "That's the darned hungriest country, bor, as ever I was in. Some parts there weren't enough cover to hide a buck louse. Their pigs were as lean as lurcher dogs; they looked ready to eat you up alive." So much, then, for the famous glamours of the East. Henceforth headless Egyptians can languish unseen for us. But about that horse now . . .

Hesitating, those before the entrance questioned those who came out after seeing the smallest horse in the world. It was no illusion. "That's a rare rum 'un; on my oath that ain't no bigger'n a sheep-dog. Do you just have a look."

We put down our twopences, and were rewarded with that which should be a reminiscence for the rest of our lives. For now, whenever we see a big dog, we will say, "Once I see a horse that weren't a mite bigger nor he—that were the year Benfield Fair were held in the parsonage meadow."

Nora, in the meantime, had been visiting another booth. She came to meet me bearing two yellowish-green vases as big as babies, and plumped them in my arms. And so home to bed.

CHAPTER XV

Now it was time for our real harvest, I suppose I must call it; our root harvest, a scrabbling, humble, earthen affair, with none of the poise and joviality of pitching the corn. No, we were like moles burrowing indus-triously among the loose earth for the potatoes the plough had turned out. The weather was fine for this, and the potatoes shone like kindly gold from amid the black earth, a scattering of bounty along the furrows for which we scrambled like the poor at a prince's door bowing before the vast autumn sunset.

"They say the pound is falling," I said as we tipped the potatoes on to the clamp; "but we shan't starve." I felt in face of that heap of crude nourishment a kind of primitive peasant rapacity, through being too long and too blindly nose to the earth. This was the coarse stuff of life, living in the earth, never seeing light. The ears of corn, aspiring and proudly swaying on their stems, were a pride and a finer pleasure to reap.

We gathered our apples too, laying them side by side carefully in straw, not only to be a winter store, but also by their flush and shine to be a memory of summer when they had hung upon their boughs. For they are jolly-looking things, I think, and when there are no flowers bring a smile of Nature into the house and hold conversations with the firelight.

The sugar-beet was lifted, but for this the heavens were opened and turned the field into a Slough of

Despond. The only pleasure I have ever found in the handling of sugar-beet has been the negative one of seeing the earth crumble easily from them. But when rain coagulates our heavy land, one can feel like nobody save the Man with the Muck Rake as one scrapes and scrapes, excavating each root from its thick coating of mud.

The traffic of carts to and fro churned up the field till the ground sucked at one's feet and turned them into flaps of clay, making one's every step as heavy as despair.

It was in the middle of this that a man came and shouted to me from the gateway that he wanted to see my cow-shed. I trudged over to him to enquire further as to his business, and was informed that he was a Government inspector sent to inspect my milking arrangements, weights and scales, as it was understood that I sold milk and butter.

By the letter of the law I admitted I did, in that I sold twopennyworth of skim milk per day to oblige neighbours with large families, and a pound of butter per week to oblige Mrs. Walter—which was all we made over and above what we required for ourselves, for I did not go in for butter-making as a business, I told him, but for rearing calves.

However, I came "within the meaning of the Act" as both milk and butter retailer, so he demanded to see my milking-shed.

"This is where I milk in summer," I said, and showed him a rough shelter of thatch and up-ended faggots in the meadow. "And here in winter," I told him, leading him into my barn, where beside the chaff-bay was a strawed partition large enough to hold one cow.

"But this will never do," he cried, gazing around at the homely old edifice with its impending cliff of chaff and its mangold heap. "You must alter all this;

189

you must build a shed with proper sanitary arrangements, lime-washed, with a drain down the middle,
and it must be swilled out every day."

Next he looked at the scales and weights and received
another shock. "The scales are old, and none of the
weights are Government stamped."

"Neither are my cows branded with a broad arrow,"
I said, rather nettled at all this waste of time.

"It's no joke," he reprimanded. He specified a
number of days—"and if you don't get a proper set
of scales and weights by then, and take steps to erect a
proper milking-shed, you will be prosecuted."

With that he jumped into his little car and sputtered
off. He was like a match continually scraping on its
box.

At the end of the period of grace I received a letter
asking me what steps I had taken to have these things
rectified. I sent no answer; and a week later received
another as peremptory as the shake of a pepper-pot.

I replied that I had neither bought new scales nor
erected a shed with a drain, but alternatively had ceased
to sell either milk or butter.

So, instead of selling the skim milk to the two village
women with large families, I gave it to them. As for
Walter's wife, she had to change from our butter to
some the grocer sells, called, I think, "Pride of the
Vale."

At last the sugar-beet was carted, leaving a field of
desolation under heavy skies. By all the signs winter
was come again, though October was hardly out. The
beet was like the burial-cairn of summer, heaped by
the side of the road. It still had to be fetched to the
factory. This the local lorry-owner did in many
journeys, which were the ruination of our lane, for the
winter. Besides beet, and for all our scraping, there
were thirty tons of my freehold land carted to the
factory. There are old and wise farmers who still

refuse to grow sugar-beet; they say that in time it will ruin any field on the heavy land. If possible, I should say that it would whittle it away.

While Walter was thatching the root clamps, one of the last local craftsmen was putting a new coat of straw on the roof of our cottage, and the one job looked to be the father of the other, for while it was in progress the straw beetled raggedly far over the eaves, making bushy brows almost for the lower windows, so that our home itself looked like a great root clamp. Then the thatcher took his shears and trimmed the thick edges of the thatch as level as a wall-top, set small ornamental straw pinnacles at either end and lacings of straw about the chimney base, and then his work was done.

Thatched house, thatched stack, thatched clamp—our cattle brought home to lie in the yards at night—sere faggots and boughs in the wood-shed—we were ready for the winter.

Here a domestic parenthesis. "Labour-saving" is a phrase in such current use nowadays that the winter routine in a cottage without any may be useful for comparison.

The oil cooking-stove, I think, has done as much to revolutionise country life as the motor-car, turning sculleries into kitchens and kitchens into comfortable living-rooms. Before, the cottage had its living-room with cooking-range, where cooking and eating took place. The scullery with its sink was probably a dozen steps away, and stone cold. Everything had to be taken there to be washed up, and taken back again. Now, an oil-stove makes the cooking and washing-up place the same, and gives warmth there too. The living-room becomes an eating- and sitting-room, and a sanctuary for the housewife from the recurrent emphasis of pots and pans.

As to lighting, from a purely social view it seems an anomaly to me that so much is spent in taking, or setting up the means of taking, electricity all over the country to farmhouse and cottage, when these places are very often lacking in a proper water-supply.

I have heard people talk of oil lamps as though they were a kind of witch-light, and cannot but think that this is an instance of modern disproportion in the sense of time-values. I was brought up in the electric light of winter London; but for a long time now I have been lamp-trimmer and fire-lighter at Silver Ley, and find the difference to one's freedom in life infinitesimal.

For curiosity's sake I timed it. It took me ten minutes to fill and trim the lamps of our cottage, another five to light them and set them in their places. Their light is kindly and efficient, and not, as some would have us suppose, dim sparks in a desert of darkness. I have never had to grope. I was the first to get up in the morning, and, while the kettle was boiling for tea, lit the fires. That took twenty minutes at most. Allow another quarter of an hour throughout the day for stoking, and you have spent an hour in lighting and heating. Would great thoughts and actions have been born in that hour?

That is not all. The other day I happened to catch part of a discussion on old lamps and fires on the wireless. One was saying, "Somehow these things seem to keep the self-starter working." That is just it. I have found that little bustling jobs of routine initiate the vigorous mood, and one turns from them to the real business of the day with a mind already alert and determined. One has done something; one will do something more. The mind needs these small things to bite on; they serve as rallying-points for the energies at the beginning and in the interstices of the day. Without them, I have found that that hour saved is spent in lying supine, and when one rises at last, behold, it has hung itself about one's neck, a great weight of disinclination.

A word about our wood fire. When I first came to Silver Ley, the old chimney which jutted into the room like a buttress had been "improved" from its original condition. It had been blocked in and contained a modern iron stove with a cupboard on either side. The stove with fire at full blast gave out sufficient heat, besides cooking, to warm the shins of one person. A mantelpiece of wood imitating pink marble, stuck upon the already plaster-hidden old cross-beam, completed the impression of mediævalism in fancy dress.

Before Nora came I had two men for two days pulling out cupboards, mantelpiece, iron stove, and debris. Three cart-loads of brick and rubble were excavated from that chimney. "Hap we may find a pot of guineas among this here," said one of the men, "for I do mind my father saying as how old Bansome what lived alone here were a wonderful self-contained sort of fellow, and no one ever did know what became of his money—for he never left none." The villager can never quite rid himself of the supposition that a solitary is *ipso facto* a miser, as though gold were a companionship excluding others. But I could not for the life of me imagine how the man was expected to have made money to store out of fifty acres; for certain I should never have a pot of gold to hide away. Though even in this the supposedly simple rustic, when the sovereign came to be worth nearly thirty shillings, had a chuckle at the expense of those who scorned him for not having invested his savings at so much per cent. It is simply that he distrusts the complex game of modern finance, and it seems that civilisation does not always have the laugh of him.

No guineas did we find in the chimney, however; which in the end proved to be an aperture resembling the entrance to a Pharaoh's tomb. Therein a platform of bricks was built, and upon it set two fire-dogs which the builder brought, saying they had been lying about his yard for years. Beneath their rust they were steel, and a fine example of old smith's work.

I showed the result of all this upheaval to Mrs. Walter, who used to "do for me" at the time. She was aghast at such a return to the primæval. All the same, this new fashion for the old had been heard of even in Benfield, for when I showed the fireplace to old Will Russet one day, in whose house was an old chimney similarly filled in to accommodate an iron grate, he said, "You know, the fireplace in my sitting-room could be made into one of these *new-fashioned* open fires like yours."

Long may Mrs. Walter continue to hate it, and Will Russet to smile indulgently.

"It will burn big logs," I said; "save a lot of wood-sawing, you know."

"Oh, aye—if you don't mind smoke," said Will.

I confess I hadn't thought much of that.

"I don't think it will smoke," I said. "Generations must have lived with it like that."

"I do," he said, accepting a glass of beer. He drank deeply, hissed appreciatively between his teeth, and continued: "When I was a little boy that chimney was open like you've got it now. An old chap and his wife used to live here then. Sometimes I've been sent on a message here by my father of an evening. The room used to be so full of smoke it fair choked the breath out of me, so's I couldn't speak for coughin'. I couldn't stay in the room ten minutes, but there they sat comfortable as you like. Regular copper-coloured, they were; sort of half-pickled, I reckon. But there," he added, "it's all what you get used to."

I lit the fire with trepidation. It smoked. Wait, give it a chance, I thought; the chimney may be damp. I gave it every chance. A wagoner stopped and thumped on the door, telling me my house was on fire. He pointed to the smoke pouring from the window.

I found that it did not smoke if a door were left ajar and a window open. But one could not live like that. I cured it by letting in a duct of air to the hearth from the back.

Now the smoke goes quietly up the chimney, save occasionally in the roughest weather. The fire is one of the principal joys of winter. It lives in the hearth half the year, for it smoulders all night, and bursts into flame again like a greeting when stirred in the morning. It is built of logs up to four feet long, and it has to be built carefully, understandingly, with due respect to the shape of each log, and repaired as it crumbles rosily away.

One sits before it attending drowsily to the small talk of the flames, till the log that has bridged the dogs all evening falls apart at last and rolls into the heap of red ash below, striking a fountain of sparks up the chimney. One rouses oneself, looks at the clock; it is time for bed.

Who would grudge the attentions due to such a friend? Not I.

The farmers' dinner at the chief inn of the county town marked the approach of Christmas. It was popularly looked forward to as an opportunity for the baiting of the M.P. To hear the "posers" with which farmers in chatting groups threatened to reduce him to guilty apology, one would have said he was a brave man to face that impeachment disguised as a dinner. "I shall ask him, etc., etc. What can he say to that?" "What I want to know is, etc., etc.—

and I mean to get an explanation." "Why haven't the Government done so-and-so—what excuse'll he have for that?"—until the poor man came practically to be synonymous with the Government—or at least with the Prime Minister—that he must answer for so many sovereign remedies for agriculture left untried.

Well, he was a brave man, for he had had experience of these dinners before. Memory conjured a picture of him the previous year taking his seat at the head of the middle table as "guest of honour" *alias* "prisoner at the bar," surrounded by those farmers who liked a dash of politics to their tillage, while the rest of us were there much in the mood of the crowd at Antony's funeral oration.

Ah, but the mellowing effects of food and beer! That had been discounted by the conspirators at windy corners. Two or three farmers may have a grievance together, and an east wind double-edge it, but it melts like a hailstone in the warm rosy common room of the inn when a hundred are gathered. Perhaps our M.P. was so far a psychologist; at any rate, he sat down laughing and at ease among us, and thoroughly enjoyed his dinner. The Fates favoured him, but did not go so far as to win his victory for him. The time came when a knife-handle was rapped on the table, and a spokesman arose.

He welcomed our M.P. to our dinner; he thanked him for coming. After a few flattering and appreciative phrases he took a firmer tone, and the gathering stiffened from grins to keen attention. We were particularly glad of his presence there to-night, for there were a number of questions we should like answered, a number of things as to the policy of the Government explained. At this point the "Hear, hear" was an earnest if not an ominous mutter. The speaker pushed his head and shoulders forward at the end of every phrase as though

oratory were but another of the physical labours o
the farm, and sat down after comparatively few words
but considerable exertion, and took a long drink from
his mug.

The M.P. rose, and his slender figure stood out among
the rest as easily poised as his fingers lightly pressed
upon the table. He returned compliment for compliment, provoked laughter by several jokes of the
right kind, and then more laughter, till the gathering
looked up from their tankards with their smiles all
ready for the next one, to find that he was swiftly
meeting those questions, not to say accusations, which
had been put to him. He was telling them in fact that
the fault, dear farmers, lay not in the Government, but
in themselves, that they were economic underlings.
That they must get together and vote in sufficient
strength unanimously if they wanted to pass measures
for agriculture which the townsman opposed. They
were taken unwary; the few politically minded were
intent upon repartees, but the mass of us cried "Hear,
hear" to his polite reminder that the farmer must rely
on his own strength, even to that political sanctuary
of a word, "co-operation"; and when he gently exhorted
us to be of good cheer, we sang "For he's a jolly good
fellow."

So the evening went off splendidly, and it would have
done the leaders of our Member's party good to see their
Daniel so at home in the lion's den.

That was last year. This year a proposed wheat
bonus came just in time for him, and though by day
the farmers professed a natural scepticism of it in light
of the earlier Corn Production Act, good food, beer,
and a festive frame of mind magnified it under the
Member's skilful handling into a golden return to
Merrie England. He received cheers on its behalf.
Curiously enough, next day those same farmers were
just as glum about it as before.

The end of Summer Time shot us into winter evenings like a train into a tunnel. "New Time," as the labourers insisted on calling it. The first few years of the alteration the farmers of Benfield refused to abide by it, and contracted themselves into a world within a world. They and their men continued with their timepieces as before, even jeering at those whose day walked an hour ahead of theirs as men living a palpable lie. The resulting confusion can be imagined—the appointments missed, the trains; and if anyone asked of anyone else the time, it was first demanded, which time did he want?

The farmers surrendered to it at last, bitterly, as one more imposition of the will of the city upon them. Even to this day you will often be given two times in Benfield. Walter, for instance, would say, "Well, sir, it's four o'clock by New Time, but by God's time it ain't but three," forgetting that He only provided the light and did not apportion it in hours.

There were rumours that Joe Boxted was giving up at last. I could hardly believe it despite his obvious plight, for he was such a Samson of a man that to see him apparently carrying the whole work of the farm on his shoulders inspired a faith in his ultimate recovery. The sheer strength of his body as he wrestled with half a dozen sheaves alone on the corn-stack during thrashing, doing three men's work, quite out-balanced the despondency of his rotten buildings. Or to see him loading London pigs into his cart without aid, or littering his stock with straw carried in on his back. Somehow one felt that he must force events to come right for him as he forced the things on his farm. But no; there was to be a sale—of what, we wondered. Of late there seemed to be nothing on his premises but mud and broken palings—except his single Alderney cow, incongruously dainty there.

"Cheer up, Joe, there's going to be a wheat quota next year," I said.

"Next year," he cried bitterly. "I want money now."

But before the sale he came round to Silver Ley and asked (this was my first intimation that he was "getting out," as they say) did I happen to be wanting another cow?

Why, yes, I answered, I'd buy his Daisy, if that was what he meant. He named a price and I gave it him, not having the heart to drive a bargain, he seemed so quiet and finished with. I enjoy as much as anybody a verbal fencing over prices with a keen opponent, but Joe had no fight left. "I'd as lief you had her as anybody," he said. "I know you'll do her well. I shouldn't like to see her go through the sale." I believe he'd have given her to me rather than that.

It was not just that he was giving up—he had been wound up. "It's a rum 'un," he said to me, "when you can't call anything you've got your own." It dazed and rather awed him, this absolute power of the community to seize, under certain circumstances, his most private belongings.

"It's nothing but a lot of rubbish," said one man to another indignantly, "a waste of time to have come all this way for." Another shook the wheel of Joe's tumbril to test it, and the whole vehicle reeled. "Ain't worth fetching home," he said to his friend. "What are the horses like?"

"Old as Adam—dear at a fiver apiece."

I should have liked to tell them to shut up; but Joe had already heard enough, and slouched off indoors. There he sat with his wife before the kitchen fire all through the sale.

Even the heap of coals in the yard was sold, leaving Joe just his scuttleful. I missed the bidding, but Reuben found the buyer and bought them of him for me. I let them stay where they were till Joe had gone.

He stayed for another week, not knowing what to do with his great body deprived of its accustomed labours. He hung about the gate of the meadow where Daisy was most of the time. When I passed he'd say again, "I'd as lief you had her as anybody."

CHAPTER XVI

THERE was a coruscation of lights at the usually dark and deserted corner of the village. Motor headlamps turned it into a stage-scene, the signpost like a lean white ghost pointing three ways at once.

The windows of the school sparkled out upon the frost, and music with a strong rhythm laughed into the stately night. The trees whispered to one another about it, like mortals eavesdropping at some gnome-play in the forest. The doorway of the school glowed upon the darkness like an unshuttered lantern. The band, then, had arrived, we said, putting heads out of cottage doors. Yes, they stood, a group of five, on a dais at one end of the schoolroom whose upper air was tangled with carnival ribbons. They played across the empty room which echoed them across the night, and before the summons was half-way through, the yellow oblong of the doorway was flickering with continual eclipse of black shadows.

It was the Christmas dance, or "village hop," which the villagers attended and the gentry patronised. The policeman and the sexton stood conversing with graven rigidity on either side the portal, and by the time Nora and I passed between them there was not only music within, but such a stamping and singing as told us that already the dance was swinging along. Yes, it was with difficulty we circumvented the boisterous current of dancing; half-way round I said, shouted, to Nora, "It is no good—we shan't get hurt anything like so

201

much if we go with it." So we danced round too.
I said, shouted, to Nora, "Let's go on; it is luxury
really to dance." For I found that I had not danced,
not really danced, since a child. I realised why I didn't
enjoy those polite dances to which the suave R.S.V.P.
cards invited one—it was because one never danced.
One moved in a conventional manner round a room,
stiff-legged, shoulders steady, hands placed so, gliding
with taut body, circumventing, politely conversing.
But here—ah! one could really let oneself go. One
could lose oneself amid this swaying forest of elbows,
shoulders, stamping feet. One could let one's body
obey the music, and dance for the joy of being caught
in a tide of rhythm, answer with elbow, shoulder, knee,
and foot, "Yes," to the music's call.

We were out of breath with dancing without restraint.
We came out of the current and sat on a desk in a corner,
flushed and refreshed by our quickened blood, as
bathers climbing out upon a rock in the sea. We
watched the others go by; their faces were the colour
of copper with red firelight on it; the men's hands
gripped the girls compulsively round where their arms
joined their shoulders or round their waists, crushing
the flimsy stuff of their frocks. Sometimes two young
men would go by dancing with each other, prancing
like young kids with that blithe awkwardness of the
goat-foot, their hands lying upon each other's shoulders
as in an impulse of comradeship. David and Jonathan.
Who would have thought it? For that was what we
called those two young ploughmen of Bob Chilgrove's.
They passed our window every day to and from their
work. They walked always in step side by side, stolid,
stalwart, of the same height and build but of opposite
colourings. One was dusky like a gipsy; the other
was red-faced, with hair all in close golden curls like
breaking buds. They never varied their gait; they
never seemed to speak to each other. Sometimes a

glance would pass between them and the schoolmistress exercising her pupils in the playground, no more—no smile, no jest. All day they trudged through the clay, through the clinging narrow furrow; and here they were leaping and laughing across the floor. How their feet freed from the native clay rejoiced in lightness and quickness, tossing their bodies into the air as though music sprang from the ground beneath them! So it lived in their hearts through the generations, from the days when the folk-dance was as spontaneous as the flowers they still wore in their caps all summer through, the old English caper of delight. For it is natural for the Englishman to express the joy of his body with a jig; his instinct in a dance is always to lift up his feet, to hop—it is neither the stealth of the Spaniard, nor the quivering frenzy of the African, nor yet the suave mid-European waltz. So when it is fashionable to dance dances imported from Spain, Vienna, or negro America, then fashionable dances are cheerless, vapid, starched, and sterile as the black and white of a man's dress suit. For the Englishman is a person at heart simple and pious; his bodily joy can find expression in the hopping and skipping of the high hills in his Bible, and in no other dance. That is why the dances of polite good taste were as a gliding of ghosts compared to this, for no matter what the orchestra played, fox-trot, waltz, one-step, these people danced the same dance to it, the rousing jig of their forefathers.

The polka was nearest to the impulse of their limbs. At the sharp spurring of its rhythm they devoured the ground in swift spasms, like bounding dogs. And if any doubt that it is the Englishman's natural instinct to hop, let him observe how a formal dance suddenly glows into spontaneity when a polka is played, and how the people clap, reeling and laughing, and shout for more.

Girls danced with girls; but while the young men capered by, run-away-with by their bodies' zest, the girls were quietly absorbed in the ritual of their steps; they noticed only the weaving of their feet upon the floor—to-fro-to-fro, wavering their skirts like wings. They had moth-like hesitations known only to themselves, moments of letting the music beat upon them unmoving, little hastes, and little languors.

Suddenly two young men would break in upon them, part them·from their self-trance, grasp them, and rush them off in laughing compliance to their strong rough dance. The winnowing of their skirts became a storm, and their uncorseted, well-defined limbs moved in lusty answer, whisking beneath the shimmering stuff, swirling it, agonising it, shaken awake out of their girl-partnered dream of a dance.

The music stopped; the girls mopped their faces with handkerchiefs, and the men mopped their faces, and round between their collars and their necks.

The band all the while had its own laughter, its own life. The pianist's hands sprang up and down on the keys as though every finger were a diver leaping from a spring-board. He looked back, laughing, at the violinist; the violinist answered, swinging over with a sudden accentuation of the rhythm; the drummer took it up with a clash of the cymbals and a luxuriant twirl of his drum-sticks, and leaned back rocking with a song. The others joined in the song, and then the dancers caught it, and their own voices increased the sway of their shoulders.

In the meantime, gentlefolk were dutifully preparing tea and coffee in the mass behind the scenes, and heaps of sandwiches and buns. At half-time these were carried round to the exhausted dancers as they sat in rows along the room. Forsaken by the music, left stranded there as by a tide, they became their bashful selves of the day, too conscious of the gentility of those waiting upon them; they took the cups and the sandwiches awkwardly, attempting to balance the former while they ate the latter.

Then the word was given out for the parade of the headdresses. But those who had but lately been lost in revelry were now ill-at-ease before the empty floor, and no one would be the first to get up. So the gentlefolk, who had been sitting politely conversing at one end of the room, rose and donned each the headdress which he or she had brought as an addition to the "go" of the occasion, with the grave deportment of those putting on their hats for a walk, and perambulated the room as though it were a garden. Captain Barkle and another, who were discussing the finding of a poisoned fox, continued in grave committee, one under the jaunty brim of a toreador, the Captain with Red-Indian feathers trailing over his back.

This hardly had the desired encouragement to the rest; but the band came to the rescue by striking up a strong marching tune, which released the people from themselves, and they rose and adjusted their headgear and paraded the room. They walked round sheepishly enough at first after the gentlefolk, but the music grew ever jauntier, and their steps responded, growing fanciful, blithe, till they had exaggerated the march almost into a minuet, and danced round, some alone, some hand in hand, swamping in their mirth the dignified upper ten.

Now my problem began; for I was to judge the headdresses. Was I to award the prizes for bizarre, beautiful, or comic effect?

There were neat hats, floppy hats, hats of sublime incongruity, hats of inspired suitability, hats that were diadems, hats that rose up off their wearers' heads and floated like sails in the wind of the dance. Bonnets, airy and deep, turning the golden lamplight to a summer's day—so many hats, martial and madrigal, ancient and modern, till even the lamps looked like ladies' faces under their wide black tin shades.

It was done at last. I sprinkled the awards as evenly as possible between the sexes and the ages. The young men and women did not take it very seriously; they were caught back into the mood of their dancing. They stood and clapped loudly when the winners' names were announced, but they wanted to be moving again.

It did not pass so easily with the matrons; they sat upon the desks along the wall, their feet on the forms, like a row of idols, figures of significance, if not of beauty. Surely our village was matriarchal, and our dance was a dance of propitiation or gratitude for birth before these our mothering gods! The wide bosoms, the deep laps, they were ranged into one great bosom, one lap.

Their old men, lean-shanked, black-clothed, and stooping, were gathered timorously near the door, as though they had been trapped on their way to church by Comus and his crew. They could not unknit their brows from the old cares of the earth; the mothers were resting in the sight of their children, as those who have climbed a hill may sit and look at the burden they have carried so far. The music stirred the young out of themselves; it put the trance of rest upon the matrons. But the old men were still at their cultivation, still stooping about in mind over the turned earth, discussing its perplexities. They were like prophets; their spirits had no true converse with any now but the spirit of the earth, ever pondering the oracle. One deepened the furrows of his brow, delving into experience after wisdom for present application. The others waited till he should speak.

But the mothers had been roused by the headdress parade; they had time at last in their laborious lives for the appraisement of prettiness. They went over the matter in great detail together; they put their heads together over the merits of each. I hope my judgments found favour in their sight.

Daughters took them their prizes to hold; all the prizes of the evening were resting like offerings in their laps. Then there were lucky numbers to be drawn for. Somebody won a cake, another an eiderdown. Lastly "Mrs. Marsden" was called. She stumped quickly through the hall, short, broad, dressed in a single severe grey alpaca garment that tried to shimmer, clasped at her neck by a brooch like golden writing. She already held an electro-plated filigree thing her daughter had won. She bobbed, and received a cushion of bright artificial silk, and hurried back to her perch. There she sat, holding the facile silver ornament in one hand, clutching the glistening cushion to her with the other.

Then the valeta. There was a sway, a hesitation, a courtesy about the dance. It was the dance of courtly retreat and advance, a rhythmic courtship. The porcelain shepherd and shepherdess would have done it ideally; but these too were gallant in their way. It was to the other dances as spring is to lusty winter. The boisterous youths of the previous dance pointed their toes and poised towards their girls. They and their girls took hands and met under their raised arms, turning back to back as in feigned disagreement and continuing a delicate step or two thus, then turned again face to face with the same grave smile of preoccupation, and swayed tentatively nearer, farther, till the whole assembly was like a field of corn waving in the wind. It was a rustic minuet; its motion died wistfully away as the music died.

Then a shout of cymbals, and it was all scattered by a satyr stampede of a one-step, quickening to a gallop, abruptly stilled by a silence and the first bars of the National Anthem.

Many hands pulled the decorations down, and the desks were pulled out into a regiment across the room. Within ten minutes the dance hall was a school again, locked and dark, awaiting its sleeping scholars.

It was sad to be sweeping up the leaves from under the cherry tree, for it was like sweeping away sunlight and the withered mask of summer. The garden drooped as with the debris of revelry, spoiled roses, snapdragons struggling still to be gay, and old wallflowers with here and there a petal stirring in a dream of spring.

In autumn it had been as though all the sun which the tree had drunk throughout the summer oozed back again to its leaves, making the whole tree for awhile an effigy of golden light. A few still lolled there, which the wind played with like a kitten; here and there on some high wand in the bare orchard an out-of-reach apple still swung, rosy or sallow after its kind with extremity of ripeness.

Yet after the nip of autumn we had a green Christmas. The verdure of the roadside grass made our decorations of evergreen look sombre, and on Boxing Day morning the air was so mild that we dressed before the wide-open window, delighting in the odour of freshness as though it were spring. This was more to our taste than to have winter's breath freezing on the window-pane. A waste of snow outside no doubt served the old novelists very well in making cosiness doubly snug within, but to my mind it is a good deal better to go out and find earth and air setting an example of hospitality in hospitality's season.

The majority of our countrymen found it too much of a good thing. "Phew, it muddle me right up," cried the fat ones, wrenching at their collars. "Dashed if I don't sweat more'n I did all harvest," muttered Walter, sitting close under the cow, milking. They distrusted it, seeing their land and gardens yielding themselves to the flattering mildness as into a tempter's power.

Boxing Day comes to be more of a true festivity than Christmas. We watched the village stirring (for the village) late, and going forth on its several pleasures. Some were for the meet of the hounds five miles away at an immemorial manor. These departed, the first relay on foot with sticks, the second on bicycles later, mistletoe in their caps as usual, but also in their button-holes each some flower that the warmth had charmed to bloom in a sheltered corner of his garden. Later still the hounds themselves went by, the huntsman and whips bright as holly-berries over the green road-grass. The majority were for the meet. It was, a local punster said, both meet and drink to him. Indeed, it was at the Boxing Day meet that the last of the old manorial Christmas might be found. It is centuries since the whole village assembled under the roof of the lord of the manor at daybreak on Christmas morning to partake of his strong ale and Cheshire cheese. But the spirit remains—at least in this railway-shunned corner of the country it did—and as far as times would permit, the great house on Boxing Day made the old gesture. The gate and doors stood open; the hounds and horsemen stood before the templed Georgian façade, and the master of the house was busy going a round of greetings, more particularly among the foot-followers to-day, for the purpose of inviting those of his own village in for refreshment, leaving the gentry to the attendance of the butlers.

It was really a day of duty for the gentry too, certainly for the huntsman and his whips; for hunting clogged by such a crowd as this was but an entertainment for the people, a parade, a fanfare, a picture of old elegance. The hunting men and women were merely pageant players. This was noticeable by the huntsman's dutiful, rather than eager, set of countenance.

Wherever they went the multitude followed, lining the roads, surrounding the woods, and applauding vociferously at a blast of the horn or merest hint of a fox.

As to that, there was always, somehow, a fox at the first covert on Boxing Day, even if the farmer to whom the covert belonged had to assure those about him that there would be, with a wink that meant he had had one carried there in a bag the previous night, and possibly scented it with aniseed to make the run memorable. This year there happened to be a glut of foxes. Too many, however, were as much an embarrassment to sport as too few, for foxes crossed the scent of other foxes and bewildered the hounds. To-day the wood contained three or four, all of which were found at much the same time. The hounds gave tongue at the scent of one, another ran back, and another broke covert in full view of the crowd. So the country-side rang with the pandemonium of people hallooing, some forrard, others back, while gentlemen of the hunt stood in their stirrups, their hats raised above their heads, each thinking the fox he had seen was the one fox in the wood. The foxes, however, doubled back from the cordon of spectators; the hounds, bewildered and excited by the maze of scents, divided into two packs, which the harassed whips vainly strove to re-unite, and the run developed into a circus round the great wood.

First a fox cantered past, and was loudly hallooed, then half the pack with huntsman and a whip. Applause. Within the space of a minute the other half of the pack, followed by the master, another whip, and the pink-coated "field," blossomed out of one of the ride-ways, deployed in hesitation, and then set off in the opposite direction from the first half. Loud cheers. Finally yet another fox appeared on the just deserted scene, apparently giving chase to the hunt. Whoops of delight.

On the whole, I think they are not sorry at the kennels that Christmas comes but once a year.

These were but distant cries in Benfield, whose true Boxing Day music, the tinkling of the handbells, had just begun. They sounded like the infants of those which had crowded the air with rejoicing peals the day before. *That* had been a general acclamation; with these the bell-ringers serenaded each house individually. It was their occupation for the day. Even as they issued forth in a body, another would be setting off a different way with a gun tucked under his arm, a ferret dangling from his hand, and such a gait and so thick deep-blue clouds of tobacco-smoke trailing from his pipe as gave him the air of knowing that the day was his for his pleasure. Younger ones were off in striped jerseys for the football field, shouting and joking, while yet another was pleased enough to sit alone with his pipe and rod on the bridge over the lake. Yesterday the rare odour of cigars floated along the village street. To-day we have returned to our pipes, but luxuriate in them, with Christmas gifts of tobacco bulging our pouches.

I had given Walter and a friend leave to have a day's rabbiting together on Silver Ley. It was a sport that had thrilled me once, but now I had grown out of love with it, preferring to watch the birds that fluttered along the hedges. The chance of the bolting rabbit strained one's attention from so many a moment of grace and light coming so abundantly to add to one's pleasure in a free-wandering eye, that the sharp swift triumph of stopping dead a flitting form was by comparison an imprisonment of the senses.

Nora and I spent Boxing Day morning simply in taking a walk. We walked in a false spring, with the banks before the cottage gardens offering posies of primulas. The warm luminous air, the breeze from the tender transient sky, seemed like a wild wish of

the earth to burst into leaf and flower. There was
only the winter corn green in the fields; most of the
meadows were still rusty with last summer's dead
bents; but the bare earth looked not barren, but darkly
fertile; there was urgency in the flashing clay furrows,
some were broken, as though lifted apart by the heaving
of life beneath. Between field and field the gnarled
trees went up like black lightnings of that liberating
impulse.

We climbed the slope to a view of the thin, bearded
hedges and dark earth stretching into the distance.
The sun-gleam, travelling it like the mind's eye, discovered here and there an emerald of old pasture, a
mirror of water, as it moved towards the church tower,
where it rested, enduing stone with the strength of the
spirit. The tower seemed to guard, as a mother her
child, its own nave crouching beside it. While shadow
dwelt on the fields, it stood shining and certain, like a
saint.

We turned and took our reward of the view.

"There," I said, as though we had travelled up
through spring, summer, autumn, "our grim old winter
country again."

"Grim?"

"Well, most would call it so."

"But not when you live with it," we agreed.

Yet it was not easy to say in what lay the cause for
our lightness of heart in that view, ragged and dun,
with seldom sanctuary of emerald green and spirit-
tower. Perhaps in the motions of the air and sky
above it. It was as though the clouds were torn by
the struggling through of the joyful light, even as the
furrows seemed shining and broken for life. Even
those most "dragonish" were wounded with brightness,
sun-sworded, sun-pursued.

Hark! A bee; and see, here a flower, there a bud.
Perhaps, as grazing creatures are said to do best on